WILD
HEARTS

CONTEMPORARY
LESBIAN MELODRAMA

GN00544078

WILD HEARTS

CONTEMPORARY LESBIAN MELODRAMA

THE WILD HEARTS GROUP

SHEBA
FEMINIST
PRESS

Acknowledgements
Many thanks to Caril Behr, Elizabeth Carola, Carla Chambers, Alison
Fell, Robyn Vinten and everyone at Sheba; and to all our muses,
including A, B, C, and above all, D.

Christina Dunhill would like to thank Caroline Natzler for her help
with 'A Badge of Shame'. She would like to dedicate 'The Green
Grass of Wyoming' to the memory of Mary O'Hara.

First published in 1991 by Sheba Feminist Publishers, 10a Bradbury
Street, London N16 8JN

Cover illustration by Pip Phelan
Cover design by Spark Ceresa
Photograph of the authors by Caril Behr

British Library Cataloguing in Publication Data
A record for this book is available from the British Library

Typeset by Photosetting and Secretarial Services, Yeovil, England
Printed and bound by Cox & Wyman Ltd, Reading, England

CONTENTS

INTRODUCTION

Great was my astonishment on being invited (last Thursday, second post) by Sheba Feminist Publishers to pen this Introduction, especially as I have never met any of these women (the *soi-disant* Wild Hearts Group) and know nothing at all about them - excepting Tara Rimsk, with whom I conducted a long, passionate and ultimately tragic affair back in the 1930s, in our *salon* days (when I was green in judgment).

I last glimpsed Tara on the top deck of a London bus, as I was sweeping through Hampstead in my chauffeur-driven Bentley. In profile behind the dusty bus window, Tara appeared pensive, meditative, even a little sad. I perceived how the years had aged my Darling. I noted the small shadows about her eyes, the threads of grey in her raven black hair. I saw how she fiddled nervously, tremulously, even despairingly, with her bus ticket.

> '.... *O she had not these ways*
> *When all the wild summer was in her gaze'*

The bus moved on, and she was lost to me - for the second time in a century. Cruel Fate!

But it is not my purpose here to bewail lost love and bemoan vanished pleasures, nor to dwell upon the shattered dreams of a bygone era. Let us turn instead to the Wild Hearts Anthology, perusing the pages and distinguishing the main themes.

§§§§§§§§§§

'Never give all the heart, for love
Will hardly seem worth thinking of
To passionate women if it seem
certain ...'

This advice might profitably be borne in mind by several of our contributors, in particular by Miss Benton, who seems (from her stories) to have a knack of picking unsuitable lovers, of the long flowing hair and flashing eyes type, living in places like Mortlake. What Miss Benton really needs, it appears to me, is a skilled *salon* hostess, who could introduce her to the right kind of woman, preferably short-haired and of an equable disposition.

Oft do I recall that time long ago when Tara and I were first introduced - we gazed at one another in love-stricken silence for two hours by the clock, missing a lavish buffet supper. *Je ne regrette rien de notre amour*, although it had such tragic consequences.

In the meantime, Miss Benton would do well to brush up her French, in preparation for Britain's entry into the European market in 1992, which should offer many exciting Parisian-style opportunities.

§§§§§§§§§§

'And love's the noblest frailty of the mind'

Judging Miss Dunhill to be a writer of considerable ability, I made an effort to interview her at her North London home - but she had mislaid her front door keys, so that I was constrained to bellow my questions through the letterbox, while she ran screaming up and down the stairs.

Fortunately I have some slight acquaintance with her housemate, the attractive and equable Ingrid of Hackney

Women's Football Team, from whom I garnered some fragments of information. It would appear that Miss Dunhill's life is no less melodramatic than her writings, and the many tales of her convoluted and angst-ridden love affairs have kept her friends in gales of laughter throughout the long winter evenings. We will draw the veil, except to say that she has now established an *amitié*, some say a stable relationship, with a talented young viola player.

§§§§§§§§§§

But what is 'melodrama'? Let us now examine the genre in which these young writers are stretching their fledgling imaginations. Dipping into Chambers and the Oxford English, I see 'melodrama' defined variously as 'A dramatic piece with crude appeals to the emotions and a happy ending (optional)' ... 'characterised by sensational incident and violent appeals to the emotions' ... '(hist.) play with songs interspersed and with orchestral music accompanying the action'.

This volume certainly does not lack of excitement, sensational incident, drama, violence and so on, and although there is little orchestral music, the characters are apt to burst frequently into song (at inappropriate moments).

This is indeed refreshing - a welcome departure from the trend towards autobiographical reminiscence and 'real life' studies that may be observed in lesbian writing since the 1890s. We move with rapidity through an array of settings, from the North American prairies to the windy Cornish clifftops. Yet London is never far away and here I was pleased to revisit in imagination a few old haunts, including the Ritz and Hampstead Heath Ladies' Pond.

The characters are active and lively, as women should be, conducting their affairs with vigour and strong feeling.

They are sword-fighters, squash players, artists, philosophers and experts in the migratory patterns of sea-birds. Withal they are frequently unpleasant; self-centred and badly behaved - such as Jezebel, the anti-heroine of Miss Benton's 'Love-All', who abandons her lovers 'with a derisive laugh'.

§§§§§§§§§§

Perhaps the first requisite for writing melodrama is that one should have absolutely no sense of irony, and here Miss Gapper succeeds *par excellence*. Her stories have the innocent charm of youthful naivety - unfortunately she is fifty-eight.

Miss Gapper's true character remains perennially elusive. She might kindly be described as 'multi-faceted' (although not 'multi-talented') - due perhaps to some deep tragedy in her past. She is apt to intone, in a strong Danish accent, 'I will never again be one woman, to suffer so much.'

Copies of Miss Gapper's first novel are thrown every year from the Clifton Suspension Bridge, Bristol, in celebration of International Women's Day (and to reduce stocks).

§§§§§§§§§§

At the eleventh hour, I chanced to encounter Miss Sandler in the Empire Tea Rooms, Tottenham, and she regaled me with useful anecdotes, between large bites of toasted sandwiches 'Savoy' and tea cakes with marmite. Miss Sandler bears a striking physical resemblance to the young Valentine Ackland. She is deeply in love with Miss Gapper, or so she tells me, and they have lived together for three years.

Their affair began in Upper Street, Islington, London N1, on August 21 1988. Upon Miss Gapper asking Miss Sandler absent-mindedly what she wanted for her birthday, the latter seized the former in her arms, slamming her against a shop front and replied 'You!' The rest is history.

Miss Sandler's writing is distinguished by its romantic melancholy and sharpened by wit. Although the youngest of this group of authors, she shows great promise - in life, as in Art.

§§§§§§§§§§

'Let's have one other gaudy night'

Dispensing with procrastination and subterfuge, I address you, Tara, as one soul to another, equal under heaven (as we are!). Through the long, lonely years - the years of my success as an author, my amatory involvements with famous poets and tennis players, the titles and prizes heaped upon me, my accumulating royalties (Empty riches! Superficial affairs! Shallow honours!) - I have loved none but you. Pen and paper now dissolve. My heart swells - the tears spring to my eyes. As if you stood before me in corporeal presence, I touch your face - I stroke your vanished hair.

Is there hope? Is it too late?

I can always be contacted through my publishers.

Madeleine Darcy De Vere De L'Isle Smith

London, July 1991

THE LIGHTHOUSE KEEPER

FRANCES GAPPER

The sea is a burden on my mind. It sounds like the voice of conscience. No, like loneliness. Not used to being lonely yet. I still miss you. Writing postcards back to London, I still want to send you one. Our relationship was conducted mainly by postcard. The cruellest thing you ever did was not give me your new address. And go on living, choose a life somewhere else, with him. It would be easier, sweet, if you had died. Sometimes I dream you died in a car accident. Or fell out of a window. Something not too painful, but final.

This part of the Cornish coast is very remote, few tourists venture down the steep cliffs into the narrow rocky bays, where the sea roars in like fury. Seagulls sweep close to me, loudly crying - too late, too late, too late.

'The sea comes in fast,' my landlady warned me. 'It'll cut you off in five minutes, less. Stay close to Peter's steps. Don't go exploring too far.'

Peter's steps - a stairway cut in the rock face, going down to the beach. Grasses and wildflowers grow in the cracks - scabious, sea pinks, marram grass - and crazy gorse bushes hang over the cliff by their roots. Living the wild life, on the edge. Everything goes crazy by the sea, even me, usually so careful of my appearance, now my dress is torn and my hair stiff with salt, I go crashing and stumbling across the pebbles. What am I running from, or towards? Light glances sideways at me off the sea. Something hostile to me here. Doesn't want me around. Who cares?

If I were a millionaire, love, I would shower you with gold, bury you in money. All in one pound coins, like stones.

You made your excuse for staying with him, your 'domestic situation', by which you meant financial - your shared mortgage, your flat, your family and what they would think. Beside these I am a ghost, a shadow of the past.

I sit on the stony beach, arms hugging my knees. The tide is coming in, water seeping up through the pebbles and the waves breaking gently, not twenty feet away and gaining steady ground. You could be anywhere and doing anything right now. Having a baby, writing a poem, making toast, making love. I am doing nothing, just sitting here. On the edge. I am waiting for something to happen.

The beach is littered with white stones. Pieces of chalk, they must be, broken from the cliffs, now washed to smoothness and rounded. The beach is covered in these white stones. And the light is so peculiar, this slanting, glancing light. For no reason, I feel scared. And cold, despite my jacket. I think, I should get up, go back. Or I'll be trapped here.

The sea meets the cliffs now on both sides.

Oh, I was afraid. I tried to climb up the cliff, but it was too steep and the chalk crumbled and slid away under my feet. The wind tore at me like a wild hand trying to pluck me from the cliff face and whirl me away. That peculiar light in the sky had deepened to yellow. There was no way out of the bay, no escape, and only a narrow strip of pebbled ground remaining between the cliff and the sea. The waves foamed and swirled below me, sending up clouds of spray, soaking me. I grasped with numbed fingers at roots, at cracks in the rock, at tufts of grass, and in this way I managed to stay clinging like a blown insect to the cliff face. Throughout this desperate struggle I had the sensation of someone watching me, but when I craned my neck upwards I could see no one, only the whirling grey clouds.

'Ahoy there! Need any help?' It was a woman's voice, strong and clear above the whistling wind. I saw approaching towards me, holding a straight course despite the tossing waves, a small boat, and within it a figure half-standing as she shipped the oars. 'Climb down!' she shouted. But overcome by dread, I could no longer move an inch in any direction, even to save my life. I had lost all strength, all sensation of power in my limbs. 'Stay, then!' she cried. 'I'll come up to you!' And just a minute later, I felt the blessed warmth of her arm around me. With her help I slowly descended the cliff and soon was seated in the boat, wrapped in a somewhat damp blanket and shivering violently. My rescuer unhitched the boat from a rock and taking hold of the oars, pulled us swiftly out of the cove, then she started the outboard motor.

As we forged through the wind and high waves, which at times broke over our bow, threatening to overturn our small craft and plunge us fathoms deep, I had ample leisure to observe my companion. I judged her to be about forty. From her face she appeared a complex, difficult kind of person, probably subject to moods and depressions. She looked wiry and strong, and she handled the boat with practised ease.

The wind dropped as we headed away from the coast, and soon we were skimming over the waves. 'You need dry clothes,' she shouted, 'I can lend you some.'

'Where are you taking me?'

'Over there' - she pointed. The lighthouse stood out clear on the horizon, against scudding grey clouds.

By the time we reached our destination, it was dark. Helping me out of the boat, she said casually, 'You'd better stay the night.'

'You live here?' I asked her. Having climbed to the top of a narrow spiral staircase, we were now standing in what appeared to be her sitting room. She had given me jeans and a shirt; her clothes were too big for me, the material rough and comforting against my skin.

As she bent over the gas lamp, a gentle light seemed to dawn in her face, softening its deep-scored lines. 'Oh, I love it here,' she said. 'It's so beautiful - well, you'll see for yourself in the morning, if the weather clears. And quiet, apart from the seagulls. I value my privacy. It's lonely though, sometimes, for sure. Since my friend died - '

'Your friend?' I questioned, seeing her hesitate. She swept an armchair clear of papers and books, and with a gesture invited me to sit. Then she fetched a dusty bottle of wine and two glasses and placed them on the table, by the lamp. When she spoke again, her voice was distant and harsh.

'Since my friend died - I've kept apart from most people in the village. And I don't write letters. Postal deliveries are so infrequent and besides, how can I write - there are things it is impossible to write. Things happen, so painful -' she lifted her hand, as if fending off memories.

'How did your friend die?' I asked gently.

'Through her own cupidity.'

'Stupidity?'

'No, cupidity. Greed of gain. But the tale is hardly worth telling - besides, you must be tired - '

'I don't feel tired at all,' I protested. At this she stepped forward and adjusted the lamp, so its flame hissed higher and brighter.

'Do you like hearing stories?'

'Oh, yes.'

'Can you listen quietly, without interrupting what I say?'

I nodded. She regarded me more closely, with a curious expression. 'You are an unusual person,' she said. 'I could take you for a child, and yet you must be thirty or more. Your face is marked by anxiety, pain - yes, I can see that you have suffered, no doubt over very trivial things - '

'Trivial?' I said, stung.

She reached out and touched my hand. 'Sorry, I didn't mean to be disdainful. It comes, you see, from living in a lighthouse. I forget how people normally talk, what is considered correct. Sometimes - I'm so alone here - I might

16

almost be living in another century. I'm glad you have come.
I - well - ' Her eyes were dark, like the night sky in the country with bright, clear stars in. She looked gigantic suddenly,
about seven feet tall, like a goddess visiting the earth, stooping down towards me. But perhaps that was my fear. I did
feel afraid. Not of her exactly, but of what might happen.
There was already something between us, a feeling, like the
knotted current in a fast-flowing river. But a voice in me said
no, I'm not ready for that, not yet. Too soon.

'But the story - '

'Oh yes, the story. Well, let's have a drink first. You
are still cold.' She poured the wine in silence, with care. I
noticed how deft she was, and graceful in her every movement. She handed me a full glass. The wine glinted dark red
like liquid rubies. 'This will give you courage, hope. Whoever she was, my dear, forget her. Don't waste your life in
regret ...'

'Well, I came here in the summer of 1982. I was happy enough
then. Drinking, beachcombing, sailing, fishing, bits of jour-
nalism in between times. I wrote book reviews, a nature
column. That paid enough, just. I rented a room in the village. Nobody bothered me. Hardly spoke to anyone. Sent
letters occasionally. The hot weather continued through
September and October, that gave me an excuse for staying
on. I was growing addicted to the light here. I hardly ate
anything, I was living on alcohol and light.

Then I met Emma. How can I describe her? She was
writing a thesis on women fossil hunters, like that Mary Ann
- Mary Anning - who discovered the petrified ichthyosau-
rus at Lyme Regis; professional fossil hunters like her and
upper class amateurs. I met Emma in the public library and
we got talking - I know a bit about fossils myself and I was
fascinated by her stories, her research into these women's
lives. Apparently the word 'fossil' became almost synony-
mous with 'lesbian' in the early nineteenth century, because
so many of the fossil hunters were, you know. And they had
such amazing, interesting lives. It's a pity Emma never got

round to publishing any of her findings - but anyway.

Well, Emma's beauty - she was stunningly beautiful - and her feminine charms barely masked a will like steel and the determination to let nothing and nobody stand between her and destiny, fame, power. Yes, she was already planning her lecture tour of North American colleges and negotiating the publishing rights to her thesis on both sides of the Atlantic. Somewhere along the line she realized, forgive me if this sounds cynical, that it would look better if she herself actually was a lesbian, or had been at some point. That's where I came in. I didn't realize I was part of her Grand Plan. I was so naive, in those days.

Well, we became lovers. That's when I bought the lighthouse, as a place for us to be together, a home for us. But Emma disliked it from the start. Partly because, though it may seem strange, she had a horror of the sea. She couldn't swim and she hated getting wet. She was like a cat, in many ways. She liked her surroundings to be comfortable, warm, safe, well arranged, which the lighthouse certainly was not. It took me months to convert it - all that winter and the following summer. Emma spent most of this time in London, visiting occasionally. I suppose I knew, though I couldn't bear to face the truth, that she didn't love me.

It never occurred to me that she might have somebody else, another lover.

One afternoon we went for a walk along the beach. Emma was uncharacteristically silent - usually she chattered constantly - and she avoided meeting my eyes. She looked like something out of *Cosmopolitan* or *19*, you know how they photograph glamorous models in muddy fields or on windswept beaches, perfectly coutured and not a hair out of place, well Emma looked like one of those models. She had fine blonde hair like spun gold and startlingly pale skin.

After walking some way in silence, we came to a small pebbled cove, overshadowed by the cliff. Emma sat down with her back to me and began throwing stones into the water. One after another in regular sequence, hitting the top of each wave as it came in, just before it broke. I stood watching her, oppressed by a terrible sense of foreboding. I wanted to speak to her, but my lips felt literally sealed, as if a hand was pressed over my mouth. After a while I turned from her, my eyes blinded by tears, and walked away - hardly conscious of what I was doing, as if somebody else was walking in my body. I felt so despairing, I just wanted to die. Before long I came to an opening in the rock, the entrance to a narrow passageway or cave. I had marked this before, but without any particular interest. However, now it drew me strongly - I felt a powerful desire to enter the passage, to escape within the concealing darkness.

Having inched myself some distance between smooth walls of rock, I found the space widening into a low-ceilinged corridor. This led by turn into a dark cavern. I could hear the sound of water, a stream splashing and echoing, it sounded at the same time close and far away below. As I stood there in the darkness, a sense of awe came over me. I felt myself enclosed in the very womb of the earth, in a hidden and sacred place. All transitory fears and pain slipped away from me. I felt naked here and free of myself, with an enormous sense of relief, as if unburdened of a very heavy weight.

I stood there for a long time, I don't know how long. I had forgotten the world outside, forgotten Emma and all that mess. But then I heard the sea, a faint echo, a faraway sighing. I remembered the tide was coming up, and no doubt the cave was flooded at high tide, I would be trapped here, I must go back. As I turned, my hand brushed along a shallow ledge, into a pile of what felt like stones, but they fell with a clashing metallic sound. I picked up one and put it in my pocket. It was flat and round. I kept fingering it on my way back, and when I emerged into the light again, I saw it was a coin. The markings were indistinct and the edges furred with mould, but when I rubbed my thumb over it, the gold shone through. It seemed to glow with its own soft light in the setting sun.

Before that time I had always preferred silver to gold, the gold of necklaces, rings, brooches always looked tacky and artificial to me, but now this was the real thing. I could understand now why men killed for gold, in the old days, the greed for gold, the passion for it, that would take them sailing long dangerous journeys and risking their lives for it, adventuring on the high seas. And maybe some women did, too. Oh for sure there must have been women sailors and pirates.

Emma was still sitting on the beach, throwing stones into the waves. I went up to her and touched her shoulder. Immediately she spoke. Her voice was pale and faraway. She said 'I'm thinking of getting married.'

'Married?' I said. 'To whom?'

'To George, my thesis supervisor.'

'Well that's strange,' I said, 'you never told me that.' Her shoulder felt like stone under my hand.

'I'm telling you now.'

'But I thought he was married.'

'He's divorced.'

'But you –' I said. 'You and me. Us.'

'Oh, that!' she said.

'Our relationship.'

'Our what?'

I sat down beside her. We sat very close, not touching, and she seemed an ocean apart. I felt like either crying or screaming. At the same time, I felt impatient. I wished we were back in the public library, back in the early stages of our acquaintance, and that she was talking about fossils, about fossil-hunters, not us, not her. Her emotions really didn't interest me. I prefer impersonal things like fossils, the sea, light. Things that just are themselves. At the same time I remembered her naked body, with anguish.

'You never let me touch you,' she said. 'How d'you think that feels? You never let me make love to you.'

'That's just how I am,' I said. 'Anyway, you seemed to like it. I thought you liked it that way.'

'I did for a while, but then it got boring.'

'Boring?'

'Yes.'

'Well, I can't help it,' I said at last. 'I don't like being touched, personally. It makes me nervous. I get pleasure from doing it to you, though. A lot.'

'Not any more,' she said, turning to me. Her voice was spiteful, triumphant, and there was a hard light in her eyes. 'Because I won't be around, see? This is the last time. The last time.' And she pushed me so I fell back against the stones and she climbed on top of me, and her hair was blowing like a golden cloud in the wind and her knees between mine thrusting my legs outwards, and she kissed me, biting at my lips and tongue until the blood came. My word she had a talent for causing pain that girl, she knew all sorts of little ways how, and especially when she got passionate, well I'd say she was like a wild animal, except wild animals are generally more restrained in their behaviour, and she was the sort of woman any reasonably cautious wolf or man-eating tiger would take care to steer well clear of on a dark night. I hope this doesn't sound bitter, I don't mean to speak ill of the dead. More wine? Shall I open another bottle?'

The lighthouse keeper rose unsteadily. 'I'm getting drunk,' she said, in the same slurred monotone. 'I always get drunk when I'm telling stories. Then I never reach the end. Just as well, perhaps. But then I can't make love to you, either, if I'm drunk. Which is a pity. Because you look nice. Anyway, so tell me something. Ask me a question. Any question.'

The sea beat against the rocks far below, a steady thudding and hissing. I remembered how the Eddystone lighthouse had been swept away, one windy night. 'Why do we cause one another so much pain?' I asked sadly.

'Isn't it a bit early to be asking that? We haven't even

21

been to bed together yet.'

'I mean we lesbians.'

'Oh, we lesbians,' she said. 'You mean us? We're harmless enough.'

'You and me?'

'No, we lesbians. Definition of a lesbian - a woman capable of making up her mind.'

'Some women make up their minds,' I said, 'to be heterosexual.'

'Yes, some do, I believe. But that wasn't what I meant. You know what I meant.'

'So we're having an affair, then?' I said, reverting.

'Yes, don't you think so?'

'Because we happened to meet by chance, on a night when we're both available and both lonely?'

'Yes, all that, and because you intrigue me. And because - but first you must let me finish telling you this story ...'

Well, anyway. Emma made violent love to me on the cold open beach, with the seagulls crying and the tide coming up fast and all the light fading from the air and the sky. The reason why I prefer not to be made love to, usually, is that it takes away my power, it drains me. Especially if it's the wrong person doing it to me, for the wrong reasons, I feel like she's put me under a bad spell.

When Emma had finished, I sat and cried. It may sound silly, but I felt something irrevocably awful had happened, and I would never be the same again. Emma stood apart from me, combing her hair and pinning it up. She looked down at me, with an ironical smile. 'Thanks anyway,' she said. 'I don't think I'm a lesbian after all. The lifestyle doesn't suit me. But it was interesting.' Then, sharply, 'What's that?' I was still clutching the golden coin. 'Give it to me' - and stooping, she snatched the coin from my hand.

'Where did you get this?'

'In the cave,' I said, 'back there' - pointing behind us to the cave entrance.

'It's gold!'

'Oh God, Emma,' I said wearily. 'For God's sake, leave it alone, don't meddle with it. The gold belongs there now, inside the cave. I don't think we should take it away.'

'You fool, you fool!' she shrieked. 'Don't you realize, this will pay for years of research!' She held the coin up with both hands, like a worshipper, and it glinted like fire in the dying sun.

In that moment, I saw her death clearly revealed, as if in a vision. I saw how she would be trapped in the cave and would drown there, alone, helpless and in terror. There was nothing I could do to save her, it was her destiny. And besides, I didn't care enough. It's a terrible thing, not to care, to be without love. I felt indeed what people condemn as 'heartless', ie literally without a heart, or having a heart like stone.

'I'm going for a swim,' I said. She didn't hear, or ignored me. I stripped off all my clothes and walked naked into the sea. The water was cold, but I felt colder inside. There was no wind that evening, it was deadly calm. I thought I would swim a long way, maybe to the horizon. And I was remembering the words of an old song, a song my grandmother used to sing. It was called 'The lost girl in the woods'.

> 'And that's where the fairy people found her
>
> As she sat weeping in the pale moonlight
>
> And the Queen bade her 'Lady come ride with us
>
> And you shall lie in my arms tonight ... '

I felt I might quite easily die, as well as her. I only needed to keep swimming for a while. And the sun was almost gone. A straight path of gold lay across the sea, tempting me to follow it. But however far and however strongly I swam, I could never reach the golden light, it was always receding from me. When I was a long way out from shore, I turned on my back. The waves lapped softly around me as I floated.

And then - and then - I heard her screams shuddering across the water, and her desperate cries. 'Help me! Save me! For God's sake, Marian! Marian!' She called me by name, that was unusual for her, and it woke something in my heart. I turned then and tried to swim back - oh God - but the tide was too strong for me, it kept dragging me westwards. Then I got cramp. I was lucky to survive that. I fetched up by Peter's steps, half drowned, and lay unconscious there until morning.

Silence. A moth fluttered round the lamp.

'Who found you?' I asked.

'Oh, a friend of mine from the village.' The lighthouse keeper smiled slightly. 'Anna. She's married now, with a baby, but that's easier to forgive. She's the sweetest person, and her husband is nice, and they named the baby after me, to placate my jealous temper. And she keeps on rescuing me, whenever possible. She always distrusted Emma. I think she'll like you though.'

I stood up abruptly, knocking over my wineglass. 'You're taking a lot for granted,' I said. 'I haven't said how I feel, yet. I might not want to have an affair, with you or anybody, has that occurred to you, at all? And besides, I happen to believe in the value of solitude, in being alone, especially after a relationship ends. You can't just rush into another affair, that doesn't solve anything ...'

Wine dripped steadily from the table to the floor. She sat looking at me. I felt ashamed of myself. Also I was feeling a sudden strong attraction to her. Awkward, under the circumstances. I concentrated on standing still. 'Have you got a cloth?' I asked, trying to keep my voice steady. 'I've spilt the wine, I'm sorry ...'

'Come here,' she said, and reaching out she pulled

me towards her and into her lap. She was stronger than me and besides I didn't resist much. I buried my face between her shoulder and neck, in the soft place where the pulse beats. Her skin felt wet, then I realized it was me crying. She smelt like tarred rope in the hot sun, a smell of boats and the sea. She put her arms around me and stroked my hair, gently. 'Well,' she said, after a while, 'it's been six years since Emma died. Don't you think that's long enough?'

'Probably,' I said, my voice muffled. 'I wasn't really talking about you, so much as myself. I haven't told you anything about me, yet.'

'Okay,' she said. 'Go ahead.'

ANGEL

CHRISTINA DUNHILL

When I said Angie and I would be together for ever, I lowered my head. I wasn't used to talking about my personal life, not used to working with confident young women who told you about theirs either.

'Don't worry about working me too hard,' she'd said. 'I like it, and I need to keep busy. I'm having trouble with my boyfriend.'

I looked up and found she wasn't even looking at me. She was staring at an old drunk staggering toward our table. He fell over the one next to it and clambered up onto ours.

'Piss off,' she said.

He reeled about cursing us. I thought, feminists are so callous; anyone can be down on their luck and I gave him a couple of quid and told him we'd rather be alone.

'God bless you,' he said.

We'd been to clear the catalogue proofs at the printers that afternoon. She'd asked if I wanted a drink as it was still early. I shouldn't have gone; I don't know why I did. Politeness possibly, or the energy that came out of her sometimes, flooding out, and then evaporating as if she was embarrassed about it. God knows, it would have been easier if I hadn't. I walked her to her bus stop and put an arm on her shoulder.

'You need to find someone else,' I said, 'take your mind off him.' The trouble was, I wanted to say, 'Have you ever thought about a woman?'

When I got home, Angie was up in her recording room already and I was cross I'd not been back in time for a meal with her and cross she'd not fed the dogs, who started following me around the kitchen, whining. After they'd finished clanking their dishes, I could hear her voice, bleak and grating like Eliot reading *The Waste Land*, then suddenly infiltrated with sweetness. It cut through my ribs.

I'd loved that woman for five years. It's always dangerous when you think this is it. Daring to put it to the test. For two years we'd hardly got out of bed. After that there was hard work and argument. But there'd always been sex. I always wanted her. And, nearly always, it was beautiful.

These days I didn't know what she was singing. Once she'd said she was working on a demo tape, but whenever I asked her about it, she said, no, she was just messing. She kept going off somewhere into her paleness. Angie had the palest hair you can imagine, washed-out lemon, that shocked against her dark eyes. I felt she'd left me somehow; she was somewhere away in her head with the song and the only way I knew she was still there for me were the cups of tea she brought me in the mornings and the way she wrapped me in her arms at night.

I started seeing quite a lot of Alex. She was always ringing and asking if I was free for lunch. Before she came, I used to work through my lunchbreaks. But I felt sorry for her and besides I wanted to get to know her. One day she asked if I felt like a drink after work. She was on her way to a meeting and had some time to kill. Now, after the last time, I'd vowed I'd never see her again in the evening but I gave in. I rang Angie and told her I'd be late; we were having another launch. She said fine, she'd got a strange new song and if I got home by ten o'clock she'd sing it to me. I wanted to rush home straight away then but I'd already promised Alex.

We walked out through the dusty sunshine to one of the wine bars in Covent Garden. We talked mostly about work and a little about our families. I suppose we were slightly more formal than usual, careful because it was evening. She didn't talk about her boyfriend for once and I was relieved. It's hard to keep patience with straight women's sob stories. But suddenly she fell quiet and I didn't want to ask her what was the matter because I didn't really want to hear. I just kept talking while she gazed at me with her chin in her hands and her fingers spread over her nose so that just her eyes showed and her ginger hair sticking up. They were very warm, her eyes. Eventually, I asked her if she was all right and she said, 'No, actually, I'm feeling funny. Do you know you've got a lovely face?'

Now, I've had a lifetime of straight women winding me up, but when she said that, my stomach fell onto my chair. I should have just said thank you but I said, 'Don't say that.'

'Why not?' she said.

'Don't be ridiculous. Because I'm a lesbian.'

'Well, I wouldn't say it to anyone, would I?'

'Listen,' I said. 'I'm going home now and I'm going to forget this. I'll see you tomorrow.'

'Okay,' she said. She got out a book while I gathered my things together.

'It's all right,' I said. 'Forget it. I'm sorry.'

My head was full of her. My bike nearly went under a lorry. When I got home, Angie called me into her room and asked if I wanted to hear it. I looked at her blankly for a moment but remembered just in time. 'Darling,' I said, 'I'm dying to hear it.'

She rewound the spool on the reel to reel, set it to play, and turned up the volume on the amplifier. 'It's weird, mind,' she said.

It was. The music was didgery-do over guitar, played with a lot of beat. It had an echo and so much space it hurt. When the lyric came in, it was soft and high.

> *If you're walking in the forest*
> *don't look to either side.*
> *When the birds start screeching,*

don't you listen

just because the woman lied.
If the trees are furred up in the forest
keep your fingers in your pockets, don't
let them dangle in the soft green lichen
where the animals have died.

I wondered if she was really going mad, 'What's it mean?' I asked.

She gave me one of her long languid looks.

'Perhaps it means, let's go to bed,' she said.

I grinned at her and she took my clothes off one by one and threw them on the floor. She stretched me out on the bed and licked me down my belly and the inside of my legs and looked at me. She told me I was beautiful and asked if I was cold. The spit was drying on my body, making lines of cold air. Where she'd spread my legs, a draught caught my genitals and seemed to move them. She opened the window, went out of the room and came back with a glass of water, dipped in her hand and started to flick it over me. The blood tingled at the surface of my skin and I could feel it going into goosepimples. She fingered the drops into stripes and started to scratch gently down my ribs and flanks. 'I want you,' she said. She went out again and came back with a paintbrush and softly painted between my legs.

'Do you want me?' she said.

'Shit,' I said.

She put her tongue on me then and I was out of my skin in minutes. Then she moved up and I hugged her hard to me and told her she was my life and I'd missed her. And she lay on me, heavy, with her chin bruising my collarbone, and pushed against me till she came, with those high frightened sounds she makes, and I held her cool ribs and pushed back her lemon hair and said, 'Oh God, baby, I love you so much, where have you been?'

'I've been feeling cold,' she said, after a while, 'cold and scared. Do you want some dinner?'

I took a bath to warm up while she made it. When I came down she was sitting with her guitar on her knee, playing a little rock 'n' roll while the rice cooked. She looked up.

'Well, you seem happy these days?'

'You're not taking me into the cold!'

'Are you working hard?'

'We've just done the spring list. We're proofing the Christmas books. It's the busiest time of the year.'

'It seems to be making you happy.'

'I like working hard. It takes my mind off things.'

'What things?'

'You and the frozen north, for one. You and the eternal fucking frozen north.' I paused. 'There's a new woman in publicity. I think she fancies me.'

'You didn't tell me there was another dyke in Magnet.'

'She's straight.'

'Oh, for God's sake.'

'Forget it, will you.'

'I will, don't worry.'

'I mean it.'

And I meant to. I was working hard all day and taking manuscripts home at night. But Alex had got in somehow and, at the back of my mind all the time, she was there. I wanted to be with her, hear her talking, hear her laugh. I couldn't stop seeing her for lunch, it would have looked rude. But when I did, I'd start to think of my hands on her back under her shirt. I'd look at her smoking, smiling and talking, and I'd just want to take all the words away with my tongue.

I started to make fun of her, flirting. She enjoyed that. When she wore trousers to the office, I'd say, 'Looking butch today, Alexei!' Then she'd swagger about and say, 'D'you think I look like a dyke?' And I'd say, 'No chance'. And sometimes she'd come in with her hair greased into waves and scarlet lipstick on her mouth, and she'd say, 'What do you think, then?' and I'd say, 'Well, Alexandra, don't try Shepherds Market, I'd stick to Kings Cross!' And she'd tell me I wouldn't know style unless it came in a packet from Sainsbury's.

But every time she waltzed into my office I'd find a way to touch her, to brush against her to fetch a pile of proof covers, to graze her hand with mine if we were looking at a baseboard or an author's publicity schedule. And she never moved it away. And then one lunchtime, she said it again:

'You know, I really like your face.'

'Pity I can't say the same for you,' I said defensively.

She looked so crumbly then, I told her I wanted to kiss her.

'Yes, where?' she said.

'Well, on the lips for a start.'

She blushed and I wondered if she knew how lesbians do it.

'No, I mean we can't kiss in here, can we?'

We finished our drinks just looking at each other and all I could do was hope she'd have the self-control I knew had left me. We walked back toward the office without a word until she suddenly stopped still in the market and said, 'Well, you know what Oscar Wilde said about temptation, don't you?' and put her lips lightly on mine.

That kiss made my head reel. I looked at her weakly but she just said, 'Thank God for that. Didn't do a thing for me. I can't be a lesbian after all.' And I wanted the ground to open and swallow me up.

I think it must have been the very next afternoon that I stopped at the ladies on my way to an editorial meeting and glimpsed her shoes under one of the doors.

'Alex?' I said.

There was no reply so I said it louder and then I heard a sniff.

31

'Ruth?'

'Alex, what on earth's the matter?'

'Can't talk.'

When I got back from the meeting she was sitting in my office with a couple of publicity questionnaires.

'Is it urgent? I'm going home.'

'Please. Can we go somewhere?'

I saw that her eyes were puffy. 'All right but I haven't got long.'

We went to the bar over the road from the office. 'He's done it,' she said. 'He's really done it now.'

I couldn't believe she wanted my sympathy. 'Oh dear,' I said flatly.

'Fuck you,' she said. She reached out and grabbed my hair and, pulling my face towards her, she kissed me full on the mouth.

'For God's sake, Alex,' I said. 'Not in here.'

I walked out and she followed me.

'I still like you, you know,' she said.

'Good-bye Alex,' I said, and rode off. And all the way home I was dissolving.

It didn't take long after that. I kept grinning at her and saying, 'Want to do anything about it yet?' but she'd just shrug or make a joke until one day she said, 'Okay but I'm not taking you back home - too much gossip.' And that was how we ended up at the Ritz.

It was completely appropriate, of course, for an affair that had nowhere to go. The only way I could tell she was nervous was the amount of work she found she had to do at five thirty and the way she fell quiet the minute we were out of the taxi. But once inside the rococo room she didn't mind my taking her clothes off. Without them, she looked somehow plumper; she had pale golden skin with just a few freckles on her shoulders. Her pubic hair was redder than her head's. It's always amazing when you see a woman without her clothes on for the first time but I suppose this was particularly charged because it hadn't happened to me for five years and this was her first time and because I was worried about seeing her at work every day - and because of Angie who didn't and couldn't know.

For whatever reason, I was overcome with an emotion I didn't expect. I wanted it so much to work and, of course, I knew that it couldn't. I was charged with the responsibility of what I was doing - taking a woman into lesbian sex. But it was love. At least that's what it felt like. I didn't know what else to call it. So that's what I did call it. Suddenly I was making a fool of myself, crying and telling her I loved her, as I sat on the bed with my skirt still on, kissing her shoulders. And at that moment, there was a knock on the door. I dragged my jacket back on to open it and the waiter just came right in with the champagne and poured it as I blew my nose and lit a cigarette and Alex pulled the bedclothes up over her face to swamp her giggles. As soon as he left, she grabbed me, laughing and hugging me hard and I knew it was going to be all right.

Sex is a mystery: a sacrament. It filled me then, banishing the clutter of everything else in my head and the ridiculously swanky room. We hugged each other tight with happiness and I didn't even ask if I could go down on her; I just did, and she made little noises in her throat and the way she tasted and felt to my tongue went all through my belly. When I came up to kiss her she was smiling and saying, 'You're great, you're great', and I said, 'Oh, I want to be so good for you, I want to be better than any man. I want to be the best lover you ever had.' And then I started crying again and she held me and lit a cigarette for us to share.

I was high, I was over the moon on her. I wanted to carve out a hole in my life to put her in. I wanted to pour myself into her. I wanted all the time in the world to be the best lover I could be for her.

'Darling,' I said, 'darling, do you think you could ever love me?'

And she pulled at my hair and said, 'Love a woman, you must be joking!'

We were both laughing and drinking and smoking and then suddenly she let her hand drop down between my legs.

'I'm sorry,' she said. 'I don't really know what to do.'

'For God's sake,' I said, 'just don't stop.'

But in that space of her uncertainty, the horror had come creeping up on me and I took her hand away and kissed it and turned on my stomach, holding it in the hollow between my ribs. Then I wished I'd never met her, wished I could undo the time, because I loved the angel more than the whole world and I'd only one life and it was hers. But she climbed on my back and suddenly she was inside me and when I tried to wriggle her out, she clung on and pushed in further and her voice went deep as she said, 'Don't stop me, you can't stop me now.' And I went weak that she wanted me, that she could do it, pressing and moving me right there at the edge of it, where it happens, like she knew all the time what to do. And she did it. I was sobbing as I took her hand away and held it and turned to her, kissing her. 'You know what you are, don't you?' I said. 'You're a fucking dyke. I'll drink to that.'

We got a taxi together part of the way home. She was holding my hand but I'd already moved away in my head. I was thinking about what on earth, if anything, I was going to say to Angie. I'd have to say something, if I wanted any time with Alex. Did I want time with her? I wasn't sure now. I thought perhaps I could make do with our work time. Didn't want to take time away from what I'd built up with Angie; didn't want, couldn't bear, to hurt her, wanted to get her back, not to do anything which would drive her further away. At the same time, I was hot for Alex. I couldn't leave it now. I wanted a week with her, a fortnight, away in bed, just taking it where it could go. That was when I entered the mire, I suppose, or perhaps I'd got swamped long ago when I first let myself respond to her. I couldn't tell the truth any more. Not to Angie, not Alex, not myself. I didn't even know what the truth was.

As soon as I'd unlocked the door, Angie was beside me.

'Ruth, I thought you'd never get back. Your mother rang. Your father's having an operation.'

'What!'

'Sit down, I'll get you a drink.'

She went into the kitchen. I followed her.

'What the fuck is it?' I got hold of her shoulders but she shrugged my hands away.

'Sit down.' She slammed a glassful of gin with a dash of tonic in front of me. 'Drink.'

I drank two swigs.

'It's a stomach by-pass.'

'What's that mean?'

'It means they're taking his stomach out.'

'Oh God! When?'

'Now. Your mother said he was just going into the theatre.'

'How's he going to eat? How can you live without a stomach? He'll die. He'll die, Angie!'

'That's why they're doing the by-pass.'

'God. What's he got, what's he got?'

She didn't say anything.

'Oh no, oh God, no!'

She put her arms round me and I tore them away and smashed her hands in mine against the table.

'Why didn't I know? Why didn't they tell me? Why don't they ever bloody ring me? How long has this been going on?'

'They've just found out. He was complaining of in-digestion.'

'What's the number?'

'You can't ring till tomorrow. I've got the number. But it's all right. Your mother says they've got every hope.'

I sat with my head in my hands.

'I know, baby, I know,' she said.

'Are they doing it now?'

'Yes, come on, let's go up to bed.'

'Fuck it, I should have rung them. Are you going to pray with me?'

'Yeah.'

We went upstairs and knelt together by the bed like two children in a Victorian painting. And when I went to sleep in her arms, there was a moment when I thought how if everybody else in the world went, I could still be happy with Angie. No one had ever meant so much to me. If I promised to give Alex up the next day, I was sure my father would be all right.

I spent the next morning at work trying to get through to the Edinburgh Royal and snapping at people. It was twelve o'clock by the time I managed to speak to the Sister. She said the operation had been a complete success and my father was just sleeping off the anaesthetic. I rang my mother and we both had a cry. She said she thought he'd be fine; he'd just have to wear a bag now. When I put the phone down on her I was walking round the office saying, thank God, thank God. I rang Angie. She said I ought to celebrate. She was sorry she couldn't get into town. I went out and wept a bit with my secretary. And just then, Alex walked up.

'I'm sorry,' she said. 'I'll come back later.'

'No, don't go,' I said, 'let's have some lunch.'

The sun came pounding down on us as we stepped out of the dark office. I told her about my father straight away and she was so understanding, I put my arm on her shoulder for a second and everything from the evening before came flooding back. I can't do it now, I thought, I'll tell her tomorrow. As soon as we sat down, she grinned and said: 'Good last night, eh?'

I couldn't help saying, 'Oh, sweetheart, did you like it?'

She squeezed my leg between hers and said, 'Yuck, never again!' looking in my eyes with hers all flecked and sparkling.

And before I knew what I was doing, I'd said, 'Do you want an affair with me?' and she said, 'Yes, oh yes, but you have to tell Angie.'

We hardly ever slept together, just a few snatched kisses in a long lunch break, and the real thing only once or twice. In the evenings, I wanted to be home for Angie. But she was on my mind all the time. If I caught her eye, I'd fill with want and I knew it was the same for her. She let me light her up; she lit me up. Every time I thought about her I'd smile. I gave her sex with a woman; it's the best sex in the world. I'd walk down the road with my fingers dry in the dust in my pockets and think about slipping them into her. I wanted to be able to put my arm round her in public and say, 'That's my girl!' I called her my little fox, she was so red. She was my virgin and it made me proud.

I'd come home in the evenings, humming, and Angie would say, 'Had a good day at the office?' and I'd say 'Yeah!' and hug her. After dinner, she'd go up and work on her music. Over the weeks, those songs were getting stranger and sparer. She'd bought a thumb piano and was laying that down over the guitar. One night we were in bed and she had her pyjamaed back to me and when I put my hand on her shoulder, she cried out as if I was a stranger. After that, she started to reject me, not always but sometimes. It had never happened before and I knew we'd have to talk.

Alex kept pressing me to spend more time with her. 'I thought we could have a proper affair, for Christ's sake.' So one day I said to Angie, 'Listen I'm getting quite friendly with this new woman, Alex, I'd like to spend some more time with her.'

She didn't look up from what she was doing. 'Forget it,' she said, 'like I told you.'

I'd never deceived her before. I felt as if there was a chasm opening under my feet. I knew I had to let Alex go. She was hurting the angel. I started to have bad dreams. A fox would come skulking over the lawn. The dogs would bark at it but it stared them out with its red-brown eyes and a bird dangling bloodily out of its mouth, and they'd be transfixed, petrified, on the spot. Alex kept saying, 'Let me meet her, let me talk to her; nobody owns anybody else,' and I'd say, 'No, darling, no, I have to wait for the right time, you don't understand.'

But, of course, the right time never came and the wrong time came too soon. One evening when Angie had said she was going to be out, I took Alex home. Luckily we were only having a drink in the kitchen when Angie came in the door. I started to make excuses but it was obvious Angie wasn't having any and then Alex went straight for it, like a woman possessed. Nothing had prepared me for this.

'Listen, I want an affair with Ruth. I love her. I won't take her away from you.'

Angie stared at her, fascinated and contemptuous, as if the hoover bag had split over the floor.

'Did I hear you right? I don't believe this. Have you ever *had* a relationship?'

'I think you better go home, Alex,' I said.

'I love her,' said Alex.

'I don't care if you'd die on the cross for her, you stupid little shit. You're not having her.'

'I'll call you a cab,' I said.

'You don't *own* her, you know.'

'Don't I?'

'I want her too.'

Angie groaned. 'Listen, I'm tired. I don't give a damn. Why don't you just do it here? Why don't you do it on the floor in front of me? Perhaps I could get off on it!'

I spoke sharply. 'Come on, Alex, come in the other room.'

'Get that shit out of this house!' called Angie after us. 'I never want her in this house again. This is my house.

Get her fucking out.'

Alex collected her things and I sat her down in the sitting room. I rang a cab and it came, mercifully quickly. She went off in tears like the evicted mistress.

Angie was slumped over the table when I got back into the kitchen. 'You're not doing this to me,' she said. 'And with her, for God's sake. You can fuck off.'

'Darling!' I tried to hold her but she pushed me away and went upstairs. I smoked a couple of cigarettes. When I went to bed she wasn't there. I went to the spare bedroom but she'd locked the door.

Next morning, she emerged two minutes before I was due to leave for work. She smelt of cigarettes and she never smoked.

'You better forget her, do you understand.'

'All right.'

'I mean it, Ruth.'

I rode into the office quite cheerfully. For the first time, I felt as if I *could* forget her. I set to work with a vengeance. There was something comforting on days like this in reducing the pile in your in-tray. I even arranged an impromptu meeting with the art director. I wasn't having my books undersold because the covers hadn't arrived in time for publicity and sales lead-in. Then I set to firming up the schedules for the autumn books and thought how much I was looking forward to getting my life back in order.

When Alex called to say she wanted lunch I couldn't remember who she was for a minute.

'I'm not asking you, I'm telling you,' she said.

I wondered whether to say I had a date but thought better of it.

She lost no time when we got to the pub.

'You're a bastard.'

'I'm sorry. You shouldn't have said anything. You dumped her in it.'

'All this time you've not been telling her. You're a bastard. I'm yours and you're hers. You knew all the time you didn't have any space. That's why you never said anything. You thought it would go away! You've used me like trash. Well, you're trash! Anyone who doesn't know what they're about is trash!'

'I'm sorry.'

'You're sorry! Is that all you can say?'

'You swept me off my feet, you know.'

'Tell me another.'

I looked down for a minute.

'Are you just going back to her and pretending it never happened?'

'I love her.'

She threw the rest of her beer over me and walked out.

I went to the ladies and rinsed myself down. When I got back to the office, I rang Angie to tell her I'd done it, but there was no reply.

All the way home that evening, I was looking forward to seeing her but when I got there she didn't come to the door. I called out but there was no reply. I went up to her room in case she had her headphones on but she wasn't there. In the kitchen I found a postcard on the table, picture side up. It was one of those stone angels in Highgate Cemetery. I turned it over.

> Go ahead then. Don't think I didn't know what was going on. You've been killing me and you haven't cared. Good luck to you both. I'm going away with a man.

I stood and re-read it a couple of times. I poured myself a drink and downed it in one. I poured another and drank that. I went round the house looking for clues but there weren't any. She was just frightening me. She'd be back later. I phoned around but no one had heard anything. In desperation, I rang her ex-girlfriend. She told me to get lost. I had a couple more drinks and went to bed. The dogs paced around the room and I shouted at them and pulled the quilt up over my ears.

Next morning, I reached out for her before I woke and snapped into the day feeling only the flat sheets crinkling to my fingers and my head pounding. I rang work and said I was ill. I made a pot of coffee and went to the living room and sat down with a manuscript. I stood by the phone waiting for it to ring and trying to think if there was anyone else I could call. My secretary rang with a query on a contract. Suddenly it came into my head that she wasn't going to come back that day. I started to cry. It wasn't fair. I did it Angie. You never gave me a chance. I switched on the Ansafone. I was crying heavily now. I was thinking of her with men. It hadn't really hit home till now.

Oh God, you've done it now, Angie, you've taken me into the cold. And it's my fault. Oh Angie, just come back, just be safe. Do it with a man if you have to. Just be safe. Just come back. Please, my darling, come back.

I went to work the next day. I couldn't bear staying round the house. and I knew I'd never be able to cope with the deadlines if I didn't. There was a memo from Alex. It said: 'Women like you are shit' in leaky biro. I tore it up and threw it in the bin.

The evenings were different. People had started to ring me and ask if I was okay. I told them I was sorry, I was just going out. I took to keeping the Ansafone on. I couldn't even bear to play the messages back for fear of it never being her. I walked round the house kicking the skirting boards and cupboards. The dogs hid in corners and threw up on the stairs. I kept them in the garden till their whining drove me mad. And every time a car drew up outside or footsteps approached the house, I'd freeze with hope and fear.

One evening when I got in the machine was making strange noises and I guessed the tape had run out. There were short-tempered messages from various friends saying, 'Why don't you ever ring back?' or 'Why do you only ever get in touch when you're in trouble.' There were messages for Angie from men. 'Angie, this is Ralph' or 'Angie, honey, this is John. Call me, we need to talk.' There was a message from my mother. 'Darling, your father is home again, but there are some complications and he's very depressed. It would be nice if you could drop him a line.'

Christ. Even when we were together, she'd been seeing men. To have ruined everything myself was one thing, but to have it ruined for me was something else. I took sleeping pills at night and worked like a maniac during the day. Over a week had passed since she left. What's more, my father wasn't better. I couldn't even think about that. Work was the only thing that kept me going. I put in a lot of extra time and worked through the weekend too. People had started asking me if I was all right but I just said, fine.

One evening I was so tired I slumped down in bed as soon as I got home with a beer and a letter pad and pen to write to my father. I turned on the radio and fiddled for the Third Programme. It went sliding through the commercial channels and suddenly I heard her voice. I heard her voice on the radio. I turned up the volume and was just in time to hear the end of the song. It was something about it being late in the day. Then the presenter's voice cut in and said. '*Hold On*, from Angie Black - going to be a smash.'

I went out to buy the record at lunch the next day. As I stepped onto the street, I bumped into Alex. We'd managed to avoid each other since the pub. I smiled weakly, expecting her to ignore me but she said, 'Hi, which way are you going?' and I couldn't get out of walking with her.

'I've got a new girlfriend,' she said, suddenly.

I have to confess I was surprised. 'You didn't waste any time,' I said.

'No point. I just wanted you to know, no hard feelings. Thanks for showing me the right direction.'

'What's she like?' I squeezed out.

'Wonderful!' she said, and I wished I had a glass of beer in my hand.

'Angie's made a record,' I said.

She stopped still. 'Not *Hold On*? That's never your Angie? Rae Anne brought it home. She works in the music business. It's brilliant.'

'Yeah,' I said. "Cos it is.'

'Listen,' she said, 'you want to tell her to get up off her arse and do some TV, make a video, do some interviews. Shit, that explains everything. She's making out she's on a spiritual quest at the other end of the world and all the time she's being a lesbian housewife in Kentish Town. You want to come round, Ruth. Bring her round. Come round and meet Rae Ann. You'll love her.'

Sure, I thought, grunting. I left her at the junction with Long Acre.

When I got home I took out the record. The sleeve was white with her face in negative and her two hands curled into fists beside it. It said, 'Hold On' in red embossed chinese lettering. I pressed it to my face and ran my nose and lips over the words. I lit a cigarette and put it on the turntable and set the volume to loud. The introduction ran all down my spinal column. It had a beat that started soft and built up slow and lazy until it swelled out. Then the melodic line came in sweet and pretty like daisies in grass, a shiny new toy of a tune, one of those you can't believe you've never heard before, it sounds so right. When the lyric started, she was singing thin and hard, right across the melody but picking up the beat. It went:

> It was winter and the trees were bare
> when you came looking for me and I wasn't there.
> The earth was hard and the birds were cold
> when you wanted to grip me but I couldn't hold
> on to love. I couldn't hold on.
> You took my breath away.
> You took my skin away,
> and all I could say was,
> 'It's getting late in the day,
> baby, don't ask me to stay.'
>
> The birds were singing when I came back.
> I'd been thinking about you and I just had to pack.
> I got on the bus making plans about us, but when

43

I opened the door, you were there on the floor
with her. I said, 'Why can't you hold on
to love? Why can't you hold on?'
It took my breath away.
It took my skin away. I said, 'It's
too late in the day, baby, and I'm
running away, again!'

I played it over and over. I was drinking and smoking and dancing round the living room. I thought, you're alive, somewhere, my angel, and you'll come back. You'll have to come back and do the publicity and I'll see you. And there was something else. I knew who the men were on the ansafone; they were from the music business. It was Friday night and the first night I went to sleep without pills.

I rang Mum and said I'd go up. I could tell she was pleased from the way she started telling me off. I fell asleep on the train with the dogs: Bell at my head on the seat and Bessie on the floor.

It was late when the train drew in and later still when the cab pulled up at the little Musselburgh street where I was born. Mum was waiting up for me. 'Go upstairs and wake your dad. He'll think he's dreaming.'

I turned around and there were footsteps on the stair.

'Well, would you credit it? The old devil always knows when there's action about.'

He opened the door, and stood, hanging onto the knob.

'So what's dragged you in lass? Thought I'd be on my deathbed before I saw you again.' He laughed so hard, he started to cough and doubled up.

I ran and hugged him upright.

'Dad, Dad, stand up when you talk to me.' I was trying not to cry. He was so thin inside the worn sweet-smelling pyjamas.

Mum took control and we tucked him in bed and gave him a couple of tablets from a jar on the bedside table.

'Did you know, Morag, the little tyke was coming?' I could have sworn he winked at her.

'Come here and let's have a look at ye.'

He stretched out his hand and I went and kissed him.

'You look a bit raddled my girl. You work too hard. You need looking after. You'll be resting here awhile. I want no buts.'

The words came up in my throat and stayed there as I looked into his twinkling eyes.

'It's great to see you, Dad.' I'd call the office and say I was ill. I couldn't leave now.

In the days that came, I tried to make it up to him. I talked with Mum. I played with my sister's kids when they came home from school and she was still at work. I had to keep kicking the expression 'in the bosom of my family' out of my mind. Rachel and I would sit up talking half the night and as often as not one or both of the kids would come down, flushed and irritable, and end up fast asleep, slumped over the table or sitting on Rachel's lap or mine.

One night she said, 'Let's go for a jar, leave the kids with Mum.' We went to the local and some of her friends came to our table and we sat round, swapping stories of the old days and the school we'd all been to. I joined in with with the tale of Mad Jenny McGuire.

She was having trouble with her easel one day in art class. Mrs Durrant lost her temper. 'McGuire!' she yelled. Mrs Durrant was a painter and philosopher; she didn't shout. We feared the worst. The class fell into a terrified hush, silently begging Jenny to fix it without embarrassing us further. Then there was an almighty crash as Jenny McGuire's easel fell on top of her. The whole class was helpless with laughter. Mrs Durrant cracked up too. But Mad Jenny went on to art school. Fancy! we said. And then to New York to make a film about women's bodies. Women's bodies! 1969 this was. She's away with the fairies, that one, we said. She'd returned to the school in the late seventies to give a talk. Legend had it girls fainted in the great school hall, she was that bold. Legend also had it she'd fallen down the steps from the dais as she left and half the hall had clapped.

'Your round,' said Rachel, and I wandered off to the bar. A band started playing and a woman a few feet away called to me: 'Mine's a double gin.' I nearly passed out. She came up and we stood there, not touching, shouting to make ourselves heard.

'What are you doing here?'

'Playing the clubs. How's young Alex?'

'Angie, where the hell have you been?'

'Seen your dad yet?'

'Yeah. Listen, are you famous or something?'

'I saw your old man. Looking all right really, isn't he?'

'The ansafone's full of messages for you.'

She smiled.

'Are you coming home Angie? For God's sake just tell me you're coming home. I've been going out of my mind.'

'We're on tour. I'm going to Newcastle, Birmingham, Bradford, Leeds. Manchester, Dublin. You can come and see me tomorrow if you want.'

'Where?'

'Ask Rachel. She's got the details.'

I put my arms round her neck but she took them gently away and left. I bought a double round and went back to my sister and the gang. My little sister could always keep a secret. I could have strangled her. She just winked at me, and we all got drunk, singing, swaying to and fro with our arms round each other's shoulders. Just before closing time, Angie reappeared from nowhere and kissed me on the mouth. 'See you at the gig, yeah?'

'Where are you staying?' I asked, but she just smiled and turned on her heel.

Rachel put her arm round my waist. 'Come on kid, we're getting you home.'

LOVE-ALL

MARY BENTON

Thwack! The little green ball resounded off the front of the court and shot back into the far right-hand corner. Dee's opponent managed with difficulty to retrieve it and propel it back to the front, but there was no power in the shot; Dee took one stride towards the bouncing ball, made contact in the middle of her racquet and killed it. 8-all, Dee's serve. One of her rocket serves. Moira could only make contact with the ball, the force of the shot sending the head of her racquet spinning. 9-8. One point to finish it off. Dee braced herself, powered another serve to Moira's backhand. But Moira wasn't finished yet; gritting her teeth, she retaliated with a drive down the left-hand side that had Dee hurling herself against the wall in an effort to get to it. A drive to the front, then a volley on Moira's returning shot, low and hard. 10-8. The match was over.

Dee ran her arm across her face to soak up the sweat, wiped her hand on her shorts, and moved over with a grin to shake hands with Moira. It had been a long hard-fought match. She liked a good fight, but most of all she liked to win.

Moving into the changing-rooms she stood in front of the mirror and flexed her arm muscles. The firmness of her biceps was matched by the strong jaw line, the long straight nose. Smiling at her reflection, she thought back to her game the previous week with Wendy, who had barely been able to return her shots, who had not made the effort to throw herself around the court. Pathetic! Hopefully now that she had reached the knock-out stage of the tournament she would meet opponents more deserving of her time, like Moira.

She showered, then moved to the notice-board to register her latest victory and see who her next opponent would be. Moira was by the board, downing a pint of Sports Lucozade.

'Well, Dee, look who you'll be playing next. That should be an interesting game!'

'What, someone good?' Dee leaned over to look at the board, then stood back, the blood throbbing in her veins. Jezebel! The woman who had loved her with wild abandon and left her with a derisive laugh. Jezebel, the only woman she had ever let come near her, utterly opened herself to. Never again would she care enough for someone to let herself be so hurt.

Her racquet dropped to the floor. She felt a steadying hand on her shoulder.

'Are you all right, Dee?'

Dee looked into Moira's concerned brown eyes and smiled. 'Yes, fine, must have had too hot a shower.' She picked up her racquet, and stroked it solicitously. 'It'll be a pleasure to play Jezebel, to beat her.'

'Jezebel?'

'Sorry, Isabel.' Jezebel suited her so much better, she had difficulty in remembering it was just her name for the wretched woman.

Moira smiled. 'Well, come on, I'll buy you a drink.'

'No, on me, the loser doesn't pay.' Dee strode to the bar.

For the next few days she threw herself into her job, tackling all the tasks she had allocated for the next two weeks. She was an efficient housing manager, setting herself clear goals and strategies and always accomplishing them. Yet she was careful to consult her staff and deal promptly with any problems that arose. At work she was well respected for her fairness; on the squash court it was all out war.

The evenings were harder. She filled her time swimming, working out in the gym. Lying on her back lifting the heavy weights on her legs she revelled in stretching her body to its full potential; lying on her back she imagined that bronzed body raised above hers, eyes teasing as the mouth came closer and closer then moved away. Dee let the weights drop with a thud, and felt a sharp pull on her back. Her body was swimming in sweat. What was the matter with her; she had not thought of Jezebel for six months. She moved to the dumb-bells, took a deep breath and lifted them high above her head. She was not going to let that witch affect her again. No, this was a good opportunity to exorcize her for good.

Seven forty-five, two days later. Dee stretched towards the ceiling. Back to the floor, round to each side. She looked over at the mirror in the changing-rooms. A calm, relaxed face looked back, a figure in a smart new t-shirt, freshly ironed shorts. She smiled. She was ready for Jezebel. She glanced at her watch. Seven fifty. The court was booked for eight; still no sign of Isabel, she must remember to call her. Typical of her to be late, come waltzing in at the last moment, go straight onto court without any preparation. She never had taken their games seriously, or anything else for that matter. 'Let's enjoy it while it lasts, then move on to something else,' Isabel would say. And enjoy it they had. That first evening sipping coffee at her place after a play, Dee caught by those tantalizing eyes, caught in a whirl of emotions, Isabel suddenly advancing, Dee swaying on the brink then hurling herself over the edge. Realizing she was breathing fast, Dee countered with a few deep breaths. Yes, she had loved Isabel for her spontaneity, but ultimately it was that, that inability to commit herself in advance, that had aggravated her most.

Eight o'clock. Dee realized she was pacing up and down the room. Damn the woman! All her careful preparations reduced to nothing. The woman was probably doing it deliberately; she knew how Dee hated people to be late for appointments. Yes, there were quite a few things she hated about Isabel.

'Hi!' Isabel breezed in, clad in a pair of jeans sawn-off at the top of the thighs, barely discernible beneath a psychedelic t-shirt. Her green eyes sparkled at Dee. 'Ready for action?'

'I've been ready for some time!' snarled Dee. She watched as Isabel tossed her long black curls back and wound a ribbon around them, watched mesmerized as Isabel retrieved an escaped lock of hair from the nape of her neck and tucked it in with the rest. How she had loved to lift the heavy locks herself, find that spot at the nape so sensitive to her lips. A shudder slid down her back. She moved towards the door.

'I booked the court for eight, you know. It's three minutes after.'

Isabel swivelled round. 'Well, I shouldn't worry, you're intending to polish me off in the shortest possible time, aren't you?'

Dee gripped the handle of her racquet. 'Don't worry, I'll beat you, but I do expect you to make an effort.'

Isabel flicked back her hair and looked at Dee sideways. 'Oh, I'll give you a run for your money.'

Dee gritted her teeth. 'Get changed, and let's get on with it.'

'I am changed. Like the shirt?' Isabel did a swivel.

'I hope you're going to take this seriously!'

Isabel gazed at her. 'You haven't changed, have you, Dee?'

Dee stormed towards the court. Waiting for Isabel she hit the ball with all her might to the front, again and again. She'd soon finish this off.

Isabel won the serve. She served a high lob that swerved down near the side wall, a tricky shot to return. Dee pounced on it and sent it reverberating to the front, so hard it slammed to the back wall. Isabel stepped forward, waited for it to come off the back, bent her knees and eased a little drop shot into the far corner at the front, where it died. She served a second with swerving spin that came off the side wall at an unexpected angle. Dee managed to get to it, but was not in position to make a winner. She rushed up to the front to intercept Isabel's return; Isabel casually lobbed the ball high above her head to the back of the court. Charging back, Dee could only get her racquet to it; the dreaded clonk signalled the ball hitting the wood out of play.

So it went on. Dee managed to win a few points, but the angrier she got, the less well she connected. When she hit a hard shot, Isabel would nonchalantly place her racquet in the path of her return and let the force of the shot work for her. 9-3, the first game to Isabel.

Dee clenched her fist. Put the first game down to nerves, now she was going to wipe the floor with her. Isabel would soon tire. She served a cannonball shot and was pleased to see Isabel unable to return it. Then the next; Isabel returned it with a clever deflection off the front wall, followed by a wily serve. Dee thought she had anticipated it, swung at the ball, and watched it sail out of court.

'Sod it!' Dee slammed her racquet hard against the wall. It split down the shaft. She hurled it to the floor and marched to the front to get a replacement. Isabel was looking worried. (Probably worried I'll smash it over her head next time, thought Dee. I might just.)

'Cool down, Dee. It's only a game.'

'It's not just a game to me, you know that!' Dee swung her new racquet wildly in the air. 'Let's get on with it!'

'I thought,' Isabel said, 'you were learning to take life less seriously.' She did an imitation of Dee, arms flailing, nostrils snorting. Dee raised her racquet, advanced towards her. Isabel smiled, smiled one of her soft, tender smiles. 'You're some case, Dee.' She was holding Dee's gaze, still smiling. Dee was mesmerized by those eyes, those light laughing eyes that had taught her to relax, to unwind. She thought of Isabel's capacity for enjoyment, which she had shared so generously, the long languid way she had made love. Dee had always been purposeful in life, gone straight for her goal; Isabel had taught her to linger on the way, relish the delights. She looked at her own hand gripping the racquet, she felt the tension in her neck. She laughed.

Isabel's smile broadened. 'That's better.'

Dee looked away. 'Look, I just can't stand the way you play, all those crafty little shots, slowing the pace right down. I thrive on someone who can match me power for power.'

Isabel raised her eyebrows. Dee felt herself blush; that wasn't true, she had adored Isabel's teasing, adored the way Isabel had empowered her to let go, lose control.

'It's the only way I can get a foot into the game, Dee. I can't match you power for power.'

'No, I wouldn't want you to. I just find this way of playing so frustrating; you turn all my best shots against me.' Dee bit her lip. Isabel had a knack of getting her to reveal more of herself than she wanted to.

Isabel turned to look at the clock. 'Okay, why don't we swap styles?'

'What?' Dee was aghast.

'Try it, just try it.'

Their eyes met. Dee knew she would have to comply; she remembered the pleasure whenever she had complied.

She began lobbing crafty balls, sending them off the side walls at unexpected angles, varying the pace with the odd hard low shot. 'You're right, this is more fun!' she cried. 'But I'm still going to beat you!'

As Dee got into her stride, Isabel fought back, matching her craft for craft, hard shots for hard shots. But ultimately it was Dee who had the stamina, the will to win. As she served winner after winner she glanced up and saw a young woman with short dark hair watching. How long she had been there? If she had witnessed her earlier slips she would have to put the record straight. Dee served another bulldozer and smiled up. She loved playing to an appreciative audience. She volleyed home the final winner, glanced triumphantly at her fan, and grinned over at Isabel. Life was good.

Sophie was standing against the rail at the top of the squash court. With each flourish of the racquet, each slam of the ball below, a shudder of apprehension swept over her. She had only put her name down for the squash league because she wanted to play different women, to improve her game. If she had been into all this savage competitiveness she would have joined a squash club, not the local recreation centre. Her first games had been against women her own standard, whom she had narrowly managed to beat. With horror she had discovered her next opponent would be the devastating Dee Donaldson, of the deadly shot and the deadlier temper. Her friend Wendy had been at the receiving end the previous week, admonished to make an effort, or she may as well not bother to play. Sophie did not think she could cope with that, did not see why she should cope with it.

Before making any hasty moves, she determined to observe Dee in action. It was not difficult to spot the distinctive mop of thick blond hair, the well-defined muscles flexing as she swept her arm back to make another killer shot. Sophie looked over at the the poor sucker on the right of the court, a woman she did not recognize, casually dressed, playing even more casually. It wouldn't take Dee long to annihilate her. But the other woman's nonchalent returns seemed to be fooling Dee. Sophie smiled; she liked to see the mighty brought down. Perhaps the great Dee was not all she was cracked out to be; perhaps if she played in a similar way she might stand a chance. Dee was certainly getting flustered.

Crack! Dee hammered her racquet into the wall. As Dee turned to march towards her opponent, Sophie caught her furious expression and shivered. She moved back out of view, taking a swig of lemonade. Then she nearly choked on her drink. Dee's opponent was grinning at her, they were talking. Perhaps the woman was human after all. They started playing again, but the intense aggression seemed to have left Dee. Sophie leaned forward, intent on the play. Then Dee looked up at Sophie and smiled. Sophie gave a weak smile back; she felt like a groupie, a starstruck teenage fan.

The match was over. Sophie resisted the urge to applaud; she did not want to feed the woman's ego. Yet she felt a surge of warmth that she was acknowledged. She definitely would not be able to play this woman, would have to be out when Dee rang to fix a date, or cry sick. Standing by the stairs, she was nearly knocked over by the next couple striding purposefully towards the court. She paused; she thought of the Assertiveness class she had attended the previous week. It was time to stop running away. She would go up to Dee, explain openly why she felt there would be no point in them playing.

'So do you reckon we can be friends?'

'Sure, after all we've ..er, been through a lot together.' Dee turned away from the force of the green eyes.

Isabel's eyes narrowed. 'Let's drink to that, to us!'

'Er, to us!' Dee crashed her glass against Isabel's, spilling the contents on the table. Isabel fished in her pocket and handed her a handkerchief.

As she mopped, she was aware of a shadow over the table. 'Here comes one of your fans!' whispered Isabel.

Dee looked up to see the figure of the woman at the rail hovering over them. She was really quite sweet, with her cropped black hair, large brown innocent eyes. She beamed.

'You were watching the game, weren't you? Take a seat.'

'Oh, right, thank you. Er, congratulations, you played well.'

'Thank you. I don't know how long you were watching for, but I was abysmal to start with. Took a while to get into my stride.' She tried to ignore Isabel's snorts. 'But what are you drinking?'

'No, I'm fine, I'll get my own....'

'Nonsense. What is it?'

'Oh, half a bitter then. Thanks.'

Dee returned with the round. 'Cheers. I'm Dee, this is Jezebel...'

'Do you mind, Isabel!'

'Oh, yes, sorry.'

'Sophie.' The woman looked uncomfortable; obviously wanted to say something. Dee kept her mouth closed with an effort.

'The thing is that I've been drawn to play you next....'

'Great! I always enjoy playing someone new.'

'Well, I don't think you would enjoy playing me. I'm not very good.' Sophie was now looking straight at Dee.

'Oh, come on, if you've got this far, you must be!'

'No, I only got this far because my last two partners dropped out.' Dee noticed the 'partners' and smiled. Obviously not competitive enough. 'I really don't want to waste your time.'

'You might surprise yourself. J- Isabel here did today.'

'I knew exactly what I was doing!' cried Isabel. 'The cheek!'

Sophie got to her feet. 'Well, so long as you don't expect much. Shall we fix a date?'

Looking at her retreating back, Isabel hissed. 'You are a patronizing sod, Dee.'

Dee gaped. 'What? I was just trying to encourage her.'

'A little respect might have been more in line. '

Dee sniffed. 'I'll respect her on the day - unless she is totally useless of course.'

Dee looked forward to a pleasant undemanding game with Sophie after the traumas of her resurrected feelings for Isabel, feelings which had now been determinedly pushed back under covers. She arrived in the dressing-room to find Sophie already there, pulling on her cycling shorts.

'Hi. Glad to find someone who believes in punctuality,' she greeted her.

Sophie looked up. 'I like to have time to prepare myself.'

'A woman after my own heart!' Dee intercepted Sophie's quizzical look, and hurried on, 'I've been looking forward to the game.'

'Remember, I told you I'm not very good.'

Dee looked away; the open brown eyes fixed on hers were somehow disconcerting. 'Yes, I remember. Well, we'll see.' Fastening the laces on her shoes, she stole a glance at Sophie. The younger woman was taking deep breaths, a look of serenity on her face. She seemed more confident; despite what she said, Dee felt she would be no soft touch.

Dee hammered on the door of the courtwith the base of her racquet. Two men staggered out, their shirts stuck to their torsoes with sweat. 'What took you so long?' gasped one. Entering, the women stuck their noses in the air and coughed. 'Why do men think they don't need to use deodorant?' choked Sophie.

Dee smiled, and sent the ball over to her, a soft stroke. She didn't feel like an aggressive warm-up today, she would help Sophie settle in. Generous to the core, she insisted Sophie serve first.

Sophie sent over a high soft lob. Normally Dee would have killed it instantly, but this evening she propelled it back towards Sophie, watching as the other woman loped forward to meet it. There was a grace in her movement uncommon on the squash court; Dee found she was looking at her poise, the way she held her head, instead of where the ball was going. The ball landed behind her in the corner, stopping dead. To lose a point so unnecessarily would normally have shaken her to her senses, but tonight it didn't bother her. When the time came she would be able to smash winners through; for now she was content to draw it out, to get into the rhythmn of long gentle rallies.

Sophie was amazed at the ease with which she was returning Dee's shots; she must have been shortchanging herself, something she did all too often. Or Dee was holding back, lulling her into a false sense of security before she really showed her who was boss. She glanced over at Dee. The woman was smiling, relaxed. Right, I'll see what I can do; Sophie started hitting low drop shots, looping the ball into the far corners. As her game tightened, she could feel Dee matching her, sending her more difficult shots, all the time stretching her a little more. She looked over at Dee and smiled; this was fun.

Ultimately, of course, Dee won. By the second game Sophie was so tired she could hardly propel her feet across the court. Yet she was pleased with her performance.

'Thanks,' said Dee, shaking hands. 'What was all that about you not being very good?'

'I'm sure you were gentle with me,' replied Sophie with a twinkle. She was surprised to see Dee wince and step back; perhaps a strained muscle. 'I'm buying the drinks today.' Dee did not object.

'Would you like to play again - on a friendly basis, I mean?' Dee wasn't wasting any time; Sophie liked people who came straight to the point.

'Yes, I would, on a friendly basis; I want to get properly fit. So long as you're not going to get bored because I'm not up to your standard.'

'No, I enjoyed today.'

They talked of films and music, their work, ideas of what they wanted from life, and found they had a lot in common. Each wanted to control her own life, each relished openness and honesty in others. Sophie smiled as she left. It would be good to have a squash partner who was better than her, could help her improve her game; it would be good to have a new friend.

They had arranged to meet the following week. Dee bounced along towards the changing-rooms. Sophie had introduced her to a whole new concept. She didn't have to play to win to enjoy herself; she could take pleasure in helping someone develop their game.

Dead on seven, Sophie dashed in, out of breath and

full of apologies.

'Don't worry, it's only just seven,' Dee reassured her.

Dee pushed gentle serves at her, adjusting her game so Sophie could return her shots. She deliberately pounded a few shots over the top line so Sophie could gain a few points. As Sophie's confidence increased, she started winning more from her own efforts, and Dee was able to step up her own game. She was fascinated by the whole process.

After one long rally Sophie leaned against the back wall.

'Are you all right?'

Sophie held up her hand. 'I'm just not very fit,' she gasped.

'Well, let's stop. Don't want you collapsing on court.'

'No, I'm fine, let's finish the game.'

Dee let her win a few points then, as Sophie didn't seem to be able to finish things off, she served a few of her whirling cannonballs, overtook her, and won. 'How about a drink then? I'm pretty tired myself tonight.'

They sat together in the bar. 'As soon as you start playing frequently, you'll build your stamina up,' consoled Dee.

Sophie smiled sweetly. 'You're right, I'm just lazy. She looked at Dee. 'Would you like to play again this week?'

She wants to see more of me; I want to see more of her. 'Yes, I'd love to. Actually, tomorrow I've got a particularly difficult meeting. I could do with the exercise afterwards.'

'Yes, I could manage that. What's the meeting?'

So Dee told her of the conflicts at work between two of her staff that she had for once allowed to fester, told her of her hopes and fears.

'I'm sure you'll come over very well,' enthused Sophie. 'You'll sort it out.'

She likes me, she seems to really like me. Dee gazed

at Sophie; what do I feel about her?

The next evening, having performed satisfactorily at the meeting, Dee arrived early at the centre. No sign of Sophie. Dee pulled on her top and gazed at herself in the mirror. No, Sophie was not her type, too young, too much like her, strong and silent. And graceful. And with such a sweet cheeky grin. Well, there was no reason why she shouldn't go for a different type. She laced up her shoes and banged her foot on the floor. What was she thinking of, she'd only just got over Isabel.

Sophie breezed in. 'Hi, how's things?' She didn't wait for the reply, seemed distracted. I must have imagined that overwhelming warmth yesterday. Dee tried not to watch as Sophie removed her squash clothes from her bag; I mustn't ogle her body. But Sophie had taken herself off to a cubicle.

'Ready now.' Sophie was striding for the court.

In the warm-up Sophie hit the ball hard; Dee responded. Watching as Sophie floated forward to retrieve a short ball, she missed the lob that came up over her head, slid down onto her back. Sophie threw back her head and laughed, then met Dee's eyes with her twinkling ones. 'Not bad eh?'

Dee picked up the ball and put it into Sophie's hand, mesmerized by the dimples in her cheek. Sophie whammed another ball at the front. She was getting into her stride, making winners; at the end of the game she threw her hands in the air. 'I won!' Radiant, triumphant, she looked over at Dee. Dee's stomach gave a lurch. She wanted to become absorbed in that radiance, that warmth.

'Come on, you're not trying!' Sophie was swinging away at the ball again, laughing over at Dee. Dee laughed back; it was all so easy, they got on so well. This surely was how relationships ought to start, not with the nervous tension she usually experienced. But what did Sophie feel?

She must get into the game. Back and forth, high and low, a ten-point rally ended with Sophie scooping the ball off the back floor and looping it back so it landed out of Dee's reach in the far corner. 'Howzat?' she whooped, beaming at Dee and swinging round, teetering on one leg. Dee reached to steady her. As her finger touched Sophie's side she felt a scorch sear up her arm. She looked into Sophie's laughing eyes. Something snapped; she was high, out on the clouds, wild and free, she was out of control, she'd never felt more in control. There was only one thing she could do. She reached for Sophie, pulled her near, felt the soft round form of Sophie's breasts against her own, moved her mouth towards Sophie's.

Clunk. She had connected with something hard, something was pulling away from her. She shook her head, trying to figure out what was happening. A sharp jaw-bone had been substituted for the soft lips. Sophie was standing some distance back, glowering at her.

'What the hell?'

It was too late to stop now, Dee did not want to stop. 'I really like you, Sophie, I find you really attractive...'

Sophie went white. 'I'm sorry, I'm not into that.'

'But we seemed to get on so well, there must have been more than friendship there!'

Sophie was standing very straight. 'I just want to be friends, that's all.'

'But you were giving off all the signals!'

Sophie's eyes blazed. 'Signals, what signals? What are you talking about?'

'The way you looked at me, the... no, please don't....'

The door slammed behind Sophie.

Dee smashed her racket against the wall. Why had she blown it?

But all was not yet lost; she rushed to the changing-rooms. Sophie was zipping up her bag. She looked up coldly at Dee.

'Look, Sophie, I made a mistake. I'm sorry. Let's forget I said anything. Can we still be friends?'

Sophie started walking towards the door. With a tremendous effort Dee unglued her feet and charged forward, blocking Sophie's path.

Sophie moved back her lip in a sneer. 'Excuse me,' and she had brushed past and away, out of Dee's life.

Dee resorted to the only relief she knew - swimming, weights and more squash. Still she couldn't get Sophie's gentle smile out of her mind, still she cursed herself for messing up something that had been so good. Lying on her stomach she put all her effort into the leg curls, piled more and more weights on. As the sweat dripped off her she started to feel strong again.

She rang Sophie, put on her best casual tone. 'Hi, we'd arranged to play squash next week. I was just ringing to check you were still coming.'

'Hullo, how are you?' The old warmth was back again; Dee's heart soared. 'Yes, I would like to carry on. Yes, seven o'clock Monday, fine.'

'Right, see you then.' Dee jumped into the air; it was going to be all right. All she needed to do was carry on as previously, stay light.

As she was preparing to go out to meet Sophie she had a call. 'Hullo, Dee.'

'Sophie!'

'I'm not feeling too good, can we leave tomorrow.'

'Oh, all right, sure. What's up, do you need anything, can I do anything?'

'No, no, I'm just pretty exhausted.'

'Can we fix another time?'

'No, I'll see how I feel, I'll be in touch.'

'She can't even face seeing me again!' groaned Dee to Isabel; she'd decided Isabel was the only person to whom she could confide her folly.

'Perhaps she really is feeling unwell.'

'Perhaps. It's a bit of a coincidence, though, isn't it?'

'Well, you do come on a bit strong at times!'

'But I made it clear I just want to be friends!'

'And how were you looking at her when you said

that?'

'Friendly!'

'Exactly! Leave her be, Dee.'

'But we got on so well!'

'Look, Dee, even if you did, she's not interested now, or she wants some space. Wait until she rings you.'

Dee clenched her fist. 'I just can't bear the uncertainty!'

Isabel smiled.

'It's not funny! And what do you mean, I come on too strong. You seemed to like it.'

Isabel narrowed her eyes. 'That's because I love women who come on strong.'

Dee's blood tingled.'Do you still...?'

Isabel raised her eyebrows. 'I mean... do you still like women who come on strong?' She couldn't avert her gaze, she didn't want to avert her gaze.

Isabel ran her fingers down Dee's cheek. 'Yeah, I'm still into the grand passion.' She turned away. 'But not with the job lot that comes with it from you.'

'What do you mean?'

'You know why we split up, Dee.'

'That was you, you were so unreliable, so...' Isabel was raising her eyebrows again. 'All right, I can be stubborn....'

'Obsessive...'

'I can change, so can you, we can talk....'

Isabel stepped towards her. Dee could hardly breathe. Isabel kissed her on the left side of the mouth, on the right side, on the line of soft down above her lips, each time drawing back, smiling. Dee could stand it no longer. She grabbed Isabel and kissed her hard on the lips, felt the responding quiver and was lost.

Sophie sat at home, watching an old film on the television, seeing Dee's flailing arms. Why had the wretched woman had to complicate things? She thought of the games of squash, forcing her to push herself, the lively conversations. Then she thought of Dee advancing towards her and shuddered. She had only just extricated herself from one situation; to be wound up again in another person, part of that particular intense tension that comprised a relationship, was the last thing she wanted. Pity it had all gone sour; she could have done with a new friend.

The woman in the film was whispering to her friend behind the hero's back. Sophie shot bolt upright. How long had the woman been fancying her? Had all this show of friendship been just that, a mere pretext? 'You were giving off all the signals.' What cheek, trying to land it all on me. Sophie switched off the television and put on a Eurythmics record.

After a helping of Janis Joplin, she felt calmer. What was Dee referring to, had she been giving off any signals? She took a swig of beer. Well, if she had it had been totally unintentional, she was just being herself. She had thought Dee was too; they had seemed to communicate openly. She sighed, then gritted her teeth. Dee hadn't been honest with her, sod her!

The phone rang. Dee's deep tones, sounding casual, trying to sound casual. Well, she is trying. Sophie found she was pleased to hear from her, wanted to know how she was getting on. Perhaps they could be friends again. She arranged to play squash.

It was the day of the squash match; the clouds hung thick and dark in the sky. As she prepared her sports clothes, she was seized by an attack of nausea. Must have caught the bug going around, she felt so fatigued. Ringing Dee to cancel, she breathed a sigh of relief; it could have all got so claustrophobic.

The next day at work, she spent hours at the word-processor. She really did need some exercise; she needed to play squash. It was stupid to deny herself something she enjoyed. She rang Dee.

'Oh, hullo.' Dee sounded distant; can't blame her after how I've acted, she needs to put her barriers up too.

'Hi, I feel a lot better today. Would you still be interested in a game?'

'Well, if you're sure. I'm a bit tied up for the next few days, perhaps Tuesday?'

'Oh, all right.' I thought she was so keen, what's the matter with her? What's the matter with me? 'Yes, Tuesday's fine. How are you?'

A low laugh. 'Oh, I'm pretty good at the moment. Something pleasant, unexpected, happened.'

They both arrived at the centre at the same time. 'After you.' 'No, after you,' as they both tried to squeeze through the turnstile, neither looking directly at the other. It was all right on the phone, but I don't know what to say to her, don't think I want to know her good news. Oh, let's get on the court.

Dee swung her racquet, whistling to herself. She was playing skilfully, yet not aggressively. Sophie braced herself and pulled out all her best shots. They were neck and neck, fighting out every point. Dee slammed home a winner and smiled to herself. Sophie gritted her teeth and volleyed the next serve into the far back corner. She couldn't stop herself gloating at Dee; to her surprise Dee grinned back, then countered with a swirling return to Sophie's serve. In response Sophie sent it soaring high, then sent a low hard return to Dee's retrieval. Now she was enjoying herself. Dee slammed home another winner and served an ace. Sophie, getting determined, bent her knees and sent the next serve into the front so it dropped and died. Dee was still smiling, but not at her; she just seemed to be enjoying herself. Sophie felt a warm glow inside; it was good they could be friends. Dee served another winner, grinned at Sophie then looked up to an onlooker, rapturously beaming. Sophie thought how she had stood, so in awe of the great Dee Donaldson. She lobbied a ball right to the back, and smiled up at the groupie. She too could share in any admiration going around. But the woman with green eyes and long black hair didn't seem interested in her stupendous shots; she was grinning right down at Dee, grinning from ear to ear.

THE SECRET OF SORRERBY RISE

A TALE OF MYSTERIOUS PERILS AND HAZARDOUS ADVENTURE, LEADING TO AN ASTONISHING DISCOVERY

FRANCES GAPPER

I was born in the southern county of —shire, a place of gently swelling hills, mild summer skies, clear flowing rivers and trees gracefully waving in the warm caressing winds. A place 'quiet as milk', as the country people say. My mother was a gentlewoman, cast off and abandoned by her rich hard-hearted relatives and yet bearing herself bravely in reduced and poverty-stricken circumstances. She took care to instil in me all the true female virtues - generosity, wisdom of mind and heart, love of all God's creatures and my own body. Above all, she encouraged my natural boldness and spirit of adventure. When I could scarce walk, she taught me my letters and so acquainted me at a tender age with the works of Mrs Radcliffe and Sir Horace Walpole.

My mother's beloved lifelong companion, whom I regarded with near-equal filial affection and respect, was one Miss Louisa Amersham. Sweet, loving spirit, may I ever continue to honour and bless thy memory! Louisa lingered on this earth only three days after my mother's death and they were buried together in one grave, in the little country churchyard, by the old grey church. Inseparable in death, as in life - their gravestone bears the following inscription:

> Stranger, below this sod together rest
> A matchless pair, and one another's Best.

Two female Friends, with but a single Heart,
who met, were joined, and never now shall part.
Cruel Ignorance begrudged their Love reward.
Nature and Truth united to Applaud.

I now determined to seek my fortune in the world. For though I took pleasure in solitude, and the healthy, well-regulated life of an independent countrywoman - quiet mornings devoted to study and philosophical reflection, the remainder of the day to hill-walking, sketching, cultivating my small vegetable garden, a spot of pugilism with the village lads, or fencing practice - yet this was not enough, could never be enough. My nature, ever warm and impulsive, demanded adventure, romance, passion. Destiny beckoned, and I must heed her call.

I decided to go North. Louisa's birthplace was in the Northern county of —shire, and I had often heard her speak with enthusiasm of the beauty of the —shire moors and dales.

While still laying plans for my departure, I went one evening to scatter flowers and shed tears on my dear mother's grave. Spring was then unfolding her brightest glories in field and woodland and by the murmering brook, and I must linger to praise and exclaim; so the hours slipped away unnoticed and it was near midnight by the time I reached my destination.

The moon was full and sailing high among fast-blowing clouds; trees cast flickering shadows over the white gravestones, like a multitude of ghosts gathering and fleeing at my approach. It was a romantic scene, worthy of a painter's hand - unluckily, I had left my sketchbook behind in the cottage.

As I stood in pensive silence, cursing my lack of forethought, I was arrested by an unexpected vision. A solitary figure was standing in a grassy clearing, beside my mothers' grave. From his bearing and attire he appeared a gentleman of means, and of advanced years. He had removed his hat and was standing with his white head bowed, in the attitude of one recently bereaved, and deeply shaken by grief. I drew closer, though hesitant to disturb his sorrowful meditations, but with the helpful intention of re-directing him to the right grave.

'Old Sir - ' I began. With a start, he turned, and gazed upon me like one thunderstruck.

'Maria!' he uttered, in a croak. 'Maria, my dearest daughter! My long lost child!'

'Nay, Sir, you are mistaken. My name is not Maria, but Abigail. Maria was my mother's name. There she lies' - I pointed to the grave - 'at rest, in the arms of Louisa, her beloved.'

'You are her daughter, then?'

'I am.'

'My dear child - ' He touched my face, with a trembling hand. 'You bear a remarkable resemblance to her. Those dark eyes - yet clear, and shining with the pure light of angelic goodness and unbending, courageous love. The sweetness of your expression withal - and your bearing, graceful and womanly. Heavenly angel!' he cried, falling to his knees. 'You are indeed her child - Maria, my own daughter, whom to my eternal regret I banished from her parental home and deprived of her rightful inheritance. She was a young widow then, with an infant clinging to her breast, and her affectionate friendship with Louisa Amersham appeared to be transgressing all bounds of propriety. But oh, that I had stopped my ears to the scandalous rumours of spiteful gossip-mongers! My dearest treasure is forever lost to me. Too late now to beg her forgiveness, to offer recompense! She is dead, and by my hand, as surely as if I had killed her myself. Poverty destroyed her spirit - destitution brought her to an early grave.'

During all this time I had been attempting to persuade the poor old man to rise, and at last succeeded. I then represented to him earnestly, and with all the descriptive power at my command, what my mother's life had been - her happiness with Louisa, the rock she leaned upon in times of adversity, their love of Nature and the countryside, their busy, active and useful lives, their devoted friends. I described my mother's artistic achievements and many successfully executed commissions. I touched, with heartfelt gratitude, on her tender care of myself; and concluding with the recollection of her steadfastness, courage and fortitude, even as the end drew near, I assured him that, whatever my mother's sufferings, she was incapable of bearing a grudge towards any fellow being, or feeling even the smallest trace of bitterness: he might therefore be confident of her complete and loving forgiveness.

By degrees, as I talked, I saw his anguish lose its initial sharpness, to be replaced by a more gentle melancholy. He stood watching while I scattered flowers from my basket o'er the grave. Then - 'Dear daughter!' he exclaimed, 'For may I so call you? Come with me to London, to my house in St James's Square. There, I can promise you a life of ease, security and good social standing. Solace my few remaining years and I will bequeath to you my entire fortune ... '

I thanked him courteously for this offer, but instantly declined it. Inwardly, I shrank with horror at the prospect. Was my free, exultant soul to be thus bound in servitude, in the petty round of London masques, routs and balls, the paying of half hour visits to Lady So-and-so and the Misses Such-and-such, the leaving of cards and the making of social chit-chat, *not* to speak of men and their unwelcome attentions? No! I had better things to do with my life. Though scarce eighteen, I had formed some knowledge of my own nature. Above all things, I longed for a Friend, a true and lasting companion, such as I was unlikely ever to discover in that false and artificial world.

Upon further enquiry, I discovered that my grandfather was returning to the Great Capital that very night. He readily agreed to give me a lift to the nearest town, King's Ditchly, from whence I might catch a stagecoach to the North. Grasping this heaven-sent opportunity, I ran back to the cottage, packed my few modest belongings - principally my sketchbook, two changes of clothes, my sword and a treasured locket containing daguerrotypes of Louisa and my mother - then hastened to the village outskirts, where his carriage awaited me.

As we clattered through the narrow and twisting country lanes, overhung by the towering hedgerows, I was filled with excited apprehension and strove with difficulty to calm the wild beating of my heart. What might the future hold in store for me? Would I find adventure, happiness, love? In all events, I was determined against ever becoming a children's governess, that well-trodden path followed by so many other heroines before me.

At King's Ditchly, I descended from the carriage into a muddy cobbled street, and bade farewell to my grandfather, whose settled melancholy had by now dispersed like the dawn clouds, giving way to a more philosophical optimism - by morning, no doubt, he would be in fine spirits. Thus - transient and shallow - are men's feelings. He pressed upon me a small hamper of food and a bag of gold sovereigns. I thought it wisest to accept, having forgotten, in my haste, to bring any money with me.

There followed several days and nights of hard travelling, in broken-down, iron-seated stagecoaches, from town to town, between flea-ridden inns. This time is blurred and confused in my recollection, and I pass quickly over it - only to say that I was forced several times to repel coarse advances from men, and my opinion of the sex did not improve.

At length, weary and travel-stained, I reached the fringes of —shire, and commanded a room in a modest but clean hostelry, run by an honest-seeming woman and her husband. Having dined excellently on roast parsnips and elderberry wine - eschewing the capons and sirloin of beef, in accordance with my strictest principles - I was shown by candlelight to a bedchamber above, where a cheerful fire was already lit. I bent over it with pleasure, holding my hands out to the leaping flames, and sinking on to a stool, I let the blissful warmth steal through my numbed and chilled limbs. (Accustomed from birth to the gentle and clement weather of the South of England, I had failed to anticipate the sterner northern climate, its bitter winds and harsh driving rains.)

Thus I remained, lost in reverie, until the fire was reduced to glowing coals and a clock chimed midnight in the hallway. Then of a sudden, I heard voices from the adjoining chamber, raised in altercation, and a woman's protest, followed by a scream. Without pausing to consider further, I grabbed my sword and rushed into the corridor. The next door was fast closed; I rattled the handle and shouted, but received no answer. Drawing back a little way, I hurtled with all possible force at the locked door, which burst open, precipitating me into the room.

Instantly, I found myself measuring swords with a man of middle age - thirty or so - in a curled and oiled wig, with cold grey eyes and a face marked by dissipation. Decidedly, a villain. Behind him shrank a young maiden of bewitching beauty, her blonde hair tumbling in disarray around her heaving bosom and her blue eyes filled with imploring terror.

After staring at me a few moments, the villain slowly lowered his sword and returned it to the sheath, his lip curling in a disdainful half-smile. 'Your pardon, Madam - from your manner of entrance, I took you for some common cutthroat or highwayman. I pray you, put up your sword - it becomes you ill, and I have no desire to murder a lady. No doubt you have misapprehended - this young woman is my niece, and I am accompanying her to London, to her father's house.'

'He lies!' cried the girl energetically. 'Lend no ear to these vile falsehoods! I am not this man's niece, nor ever will be - merely his third, fourth, or perchance even fifth cousin - and he has no natural authority, nor any rights over me. Were it not that I foolishly, without consideration - that I - ' whereupon she burst into a shower of tears.

Her honour was clearly at stake, and mine also; for I took some pride in my swordsmanship, and was enraged by the man's insults. 'Never fear!' I cried. 'I am your sister, and will defend you to the death, if need be. Sir, I challenge you!' I thrust forward, ripping open his waistcoat. He flinched back in surprise, his eyes narrowing, and emitted a sound not unlike a hiss from between clenched teeth. We fought up and down the room, our swords flashing in the candlelight. I had the initial advantage of surprise, but was hampered by my dress; nevertheless, I had benefited from Louisa's instruction, and she was an excellent swordswoman. I was beginning to gain the upper hand, when he leapt behind a small table, kicking it towards me so that I stumbled over it - then, while I was still regaining my balance, he pinked me in the arm.

I fought on bravely with my left hand, and at length, with a cunning twist, sent his sword spinning across the room. 'Mercy!' he cried, falling on his knees before me.

'You deserve none,' I answered. 'But nevertheless, I will spare your life - on condition that you first apologize to this lady, for attempting to force your unwelcome attentions upon her, and then leave this place instantly ... '

With a sideways glance in her direction, he muttered something below his breath, the substance of which I construed as an apology, although the words were impossible to distinguish - then rose heavily and stumbled from the room. I kicked the door shut behind him.

Then turned.

Her eyes were heavenly blue, like summer skies, her skin so astonishingly fair and clear, it seemed almost transparent, her hair loosened of its bindings seemed to float around her like a shining golden mist. Her dress was of sprigged muslin, caught under her breasts with a ribbon, accentuating their soft fullness. Her mouth was like a cherry. Her nose was simple but charming. The speaking blood rose to her cheeks as I gazed upon her, imparting to them a delicate tinge, like a white rose flushed with the faintest hue of pink. A rose, I thought, just unfurled from the bud - with the fresh early morning dew not yet evaporated from her soft, velvety petals - fragrant, innocent, untouched. As I stood captured by admiration, she sighed and spoke. Her voice was clear and musical, yet low, and it thrilled me to the depths, to the very marrow, to my innermost soul. The precise words at first escaped me, so entranced was I, but at length I absorbed them.

'Now I suppose you, too, have fallen in love with me!' she exclaimed, in disconsolate, impatient tones. 'Oh yes, don't trouble to deny it. I perceive the signs already - your moonstruck eyes and that foolish expression upon your face.

Oh, why does this always .... '

Her voice was drowned by a loud commotion from the yard below - the snorting and alarmed neighing of horses, clattering on the cobbles, and a man's voice - that of my former opponent - uttering a string of voluble curses. 'Damn you, Horace, let go! You'll ruin the creature's mouth! Here, take this!' - the sharp ringing of coins on stone.

My companion rushed to the window, and leaning out, cried 'Stop him! Landlord, I charge you!' - then, as the sound of hooves faded, she uttered a despairing cry. 'Oh God, he has stolen her! My dearest Belinda!'

She fell back, and threw herself on the bed, in a fury of impatient anguish.

'Who is Belinda?' I inquired.

'My horse, my sweet horse!'

'Are you very fond of her, then?'

'Oh, you have no conception! She means everything to me! She has all my heart! And now Roland - my wicked cousin - has ravished her from me!' And she burst once more into hysterical tears.

I made inarticulate sounds of sympathy, for her distress could not but move me, although personally I never had much of a fondness for horses. She raised her head and gazed at me, her eyes like drowned violets in a lake of milk. 'I entreat you, go after him! Pursue him, the dastard! We must lose no time. Every second is precious - I am sure the landlord, honest Horace, would willingly lend you one of his horses ... '

The room faded and grew dim, and my ears were filled with an immense roaring, like the sea or like wind sweeping over the hills. 'Your pardon - at this moment I cannot - ' I heard my voice coming as if from a long way off, and her dismayed exclamation - 'Oh God, what is it? Your sleeve is soaked with blood! You are wounded!' Then I lost consciousness.

When I awoke, I was lying on a soft bed, near a shuttered window. I could see bright sunlight between the slats, and birds were singing musically outside. 'Where am I?' was my first thought, then as memory flooded back, 'and where is she? How long have I been lying here, unconscious, and what has transpired in the interval? Has that villain returned to abduct her, to force her against her will? Has he killed her? Alas the day!'

I struggled to rise, and at once sank back, overcome by dizziness. My arm was tightly bandaged, past the elbow, so I could scarcely move it; even my hand felt numb. Gazing round me, I saw my dress and undergarments laid over a chair. A clock ticked on the mantelpiece, above a fireplace heaped with grey ashes. A moment later, I heard a soft tread; the door-handle turned and the innkeeper entered. A smile spread across her face on seeing me; approaching, she laid a cool hand on my forehead.

'How are you faring?' she enquired.

'Madam, I beseech you tell me, how long have I been lying here?'

'Three days and more. The fever has passed, thanks be.'

'Where is the young lady who –'

'Whish, settle back now. She's long gone. She paid her account and rushed away like the wind in a great hurry – I doubt you'll ever catch up with her. But stay – now I recall, she left a letter for you –'

Stepping out of the room, she returned a moment later, holding a sealed document, tied up with ribands; this she extended towards me at arm's length and with a somewhat doubtful air. 'Pray, fold back the shutters...' I implored. She did so, and the morning sunlight flooded in. I tore open the letter and eagerly devoured it, although the hand was near indecipherable: but at length I made out the following:

My dear Friend,

Forgive my discourtesy towards you: it was ill judged. The desperation of my predicament having raised my emotions to fever pitch, I can hardly be held

while those around me were dying of thirst ...

But this, though bad enough, was not the limit of my sorrowful predicament. Scarce twelve years old, I was acknowledged universally as a Beauty, and receiving homage from all sides. Everybody I met seemed to fall in love with me - one gentleman, madly enamoured and attempting to scale the wall to my bedchamber, fell from a drainpipe and was killed; another, a melancholiac, drowned himself; several were slain or horribly injured in duels; and so on. By my fifteenth year, I had received three times that many proposals of marriage, and suffered countless insults and indecent suggestions.

And not only from men! Nay, though innocently I had fled for protection and safety to the female sex, I soon discovered the naivety of my conceptions. One governess after the other had to be dismissed without a character - cooks and kitchenmaids likewise. Even my aunt, a highly respectable married woman, made advances to me in the shrubbery, when she and I were sheltering from a rainstorm.

At last, my only place of refuge was the stables, where the groom and stable lad were happily enamoured only of one another; and there I first encountered my beloved Belinda. Horses are in every way preferable to human beings, I consider: their odour is sweeter, their intelligence more sensitive and refined; above all they are utterly indifferent to foolish aesthetic considerations. Belinda has no notion of my being beautiful or charming: she likes me because I feed her with apples and keep a light hand on the reins. I honour her judgement. She herself is a peculiarly ugly horse; but no words of mine can describe the sweetness and gaiety of her spirit. I cannot help but shed a tear, remembering. Forgive the brevity of this communication. I must depart instantly, in pursuit of Roland, my wicked cousin, for I feel sure he intends harm to Belinda.

Adieu - Marianne.

Having perused the forgoing epistle, I refolded it with a sigh, and fell back. 'Well, there is no use in following her, even if I were capable of doing so. Marianne!' - I breathed the lovely name aloud.

'Marianne!' echoed a mocking voice, behind me. I turned sharply, and saw to my utter astonishment and confusion, standing by my bedstead, a man! Though apparently a mere stripling, not more than eighteen, his manner was self-assured and easy - he seemed not in the least discomfited by my horrified gaze.

In stature he was of middle height, and slim. His hair was a light reddish brown, tied back with a riband and powdered. He wore a brown velvet coat, with darker lacing, and a cambric shirt, with a lace neck-cloth, falling in lavish ruffles. This modish style of dress gave him a somewhat foppish air, belied by the sword fastened neatly at his side. Also the swiftness of his movements - for before I knew it, he was gone from behind me and arranging himself comfortably on the broad window seat. His shapely legs were clad in white stockings and buckled shoes.

'Who is Marianne? Your sister, cousin, friend, mistress?'

A pang shot to my heart at the latter suggestion, but I bit my lip and strove to maintain a stony expression. 'I wonder, Sir, that you should make it your business to enquire. Marianne is - a stranger to me - I encountered her but recently, and we parted not half an hour after meeting.'

'Is that so?' His brow lifted and his gaze rested upon me, thoughtfully. 'And will you - ah - encounter her again, in the foreseeable future?'

'How should I tell?' was my irritable rejoinder.

'I merely wondered.'

'And I can only repeat, what business may it be of yours?'

'None at all - unless I should perchance take an interest in your affairs, and choose to involve myself therein.'

'Pray desist from doing so. I would rather you left me - and my affairs - entirely alone.' Unwisely, I made an abrupt movement, and winced.

'That arm is dressed very clumsily - no wonder it pains you. I understand something of physic - will you allow me - ?' Before I could protest, he was at my side, untying the bandage. A faintness overcame me and my sight was dimmed for a moment: I heard his sharply indrawn breath on seeing the wound. 'This must be cleaned, and the dressing renewed.'

'No, I pray you - ' I protested, weakly.

'My dear girl, you can trust my discretion, calm yourself.'

'But I would rather have a woman - '

'I admire your discrimination. However, this is hardly the time to be debating the merits of the sexes ...'

These were the last words I heard; then I must have lapsed into unconsciousness, for when I next opened my eyes, he was gone.

I had slept deeply, and was filled with the sweetest sensation of peace, as if rocked gently and hushed in my own dear mother's arms. It was evening, and the moon cast down her luminous beams, suffusing my chamber with a soft radiance. Instantly I rose and walked to the window. My arm was loosely bound and no longer troubled me, although I was greatly weakened by the fever, and somewhat dazed by the rapid passing of recent events. 'That extraordinary young man - who was he, I wonder? Did I dream of him, or does he exist in truth? Sure, I could never have imagined such a vision!' I smiled, remembering. 'Despite his discourtesy, I liked him. He amused me and he was charming, unlike other men. I wonder if ... '

I settled myself in the broad window enclosure, gazing out across the moonlit fields; and sighed deeply. 'How ignorant I am! I understand nothing of man, or woman either. My own heart is an entire mystery to me. I have travelled far, yet for no good cause, and to no perceptible end - my destination becomes increasingly uncertain, ever retreating as I advance. Where shall I find true happiness? Am I wrong in settling my hopes on that elusive object - should I not rather strive to curb and restrain my perhaps too impulsive, too eager nature; by turning inwards, to rely ever more upon myself, establishing a surer foundation of self-knowledge and moral strength? Since I am now alone in the world, with none to care for me and nobody to love, and no reason to expect any change in this most painful predicament. Nay, since I fall in love so easily and on such slender acquaintance, it may be that I am incapable of forming any lasting attachment ...'

Thus beseiged by melancholy thoughts, and plunging ever deeper into self-induced despondency, I sat and wept; till of a sudden, some other influence, of relief, of comfort, seemed to enter my soul. I lifted my eyes and saw before me a vision - the face of a woman, old and wise - neither Louisa nor my mother, yet with something of each in her countenance.

'Arise, my daughter!' she exclaimed. 'Forgo these bitter doubts and needless self-recriminations. Never doubt your capacity to love, and that you will receive abundant love in return. There is one who needs you and who is in peril of her life. You alone have the power to save her. Take courage, therefore, and struggle onward ...'

Her face shimmered and vanished. I was left alone, gazing at the blank and rounded full moon. Yet in spirit I was no longer alone - no longer despairing or wrought upon by the false phantoms of tremulous conscience. 'So be it!' I exclaimed. 'Great Mother of All, how can I choose but obey you, and follow rejoicing wherever you direct me?' And I passed several moments in silent thankfulness.

Pangs of hunger then assailed me, and recollecting that I had eaten nothing for nigh on three days, I dressed myself and hastened downstairs. I could discover little of sustenance in the larder, saving a number of dry biscuits, which I consumed with an eager appetite. Then, throwing a thick cloak over my shoulders, I drew the bolts of a side door, and stepped into the cobbled courtyard.

Dawn was then stretching her yellow fingers across the eastern horizon, and the joyous calling of birds rang clearly on the still air. A cock crew; a dog barked; deep sighs and impatient blowing noises came from the nearby stables. Taking a circuit of the building, I admired how the hillside rose up steeply and majestically behind; the little inn seeming to nestle in its depths, like a chick folded under her mother's wing. This situation would account, I reflected, for the extreme dampness of the structure, and the resultant gloomy and dank atmosphere of the lower rooms - 'it be all thikky up the walls', as my countrymen would say.

Well, I had reached the North, and was already enchanted by it. Life moved here at an exhilarating pace; the very air seemed infused with passion and adventure; soon I hoped to make acquaintances less transient, or even friends. Though doubtless many of these —shire folk, as in other remote country places, would be dour and distrustful of strangers. On this point, I determined to interrogate my good hostess, whom by her quaint accents and turn of speech I judged a —shire woman born and bred. A moment later, I heard a stirring within the house and she emerged, throwing a bucket of slops into the courtyard.

She greeted me, though with a sober mien, and an air of heaviness - I hardly recognized my comforter of the previous morning. Without further preamble, she began 'You'll not have heard - and the tidings will hardly touch thee, being a foreigner -'

'What, I pray you?'

She drew closer to me, lowering her voice and casting a nervous glance back over her shoulder, as if wary of intruders. 'A man was killed last night, crushed to death by a falling rock, as he was riding homewards, along by Carransfell ...'

A cold chill struck to my heart, recalling my visitor, that young man of the lace ruffles and exquisite manners. I described him to my hostess, and she regarded me with astonishment. 'Know you not who that was? 'Twas Lord Courtenay de L'Isle. From the concern he showed over thee, I felt sure he must be thy cousin or some other relative. No, 'twas not he, but —, a well-to-do farmer of this district ...'

On further enquiry, I elicited the following sensational information: it appeared that this part of —shire was
greatly infested with foot robbers; the roads being narrow
and not seldom overhung by steep ledged outcrops of rock,
these desperados would leap down from above on passing
carriages; then, having disabled the coachmen and stripped
those within of money and valuables, they would scatter and
vanish into the surrounding hills.

However, the terrain was in general bare and bleak,
offering few hiding places; or it turned quickly from rocky
crags to open moorland. To forestall pursuers, the robbers
had lately adopted a most cruel and dastardly practice. One
of their number would remain above, overlooking the scene,
and on a pre-arranged signal, would send rocks of a massive
size tumbling and bouncing down the hillside. These would
oftentimes hurt or kill innocent travellers, or else fright the
horses, causing them to bolt; or set off a landslide, crushing
all below and blocking the road for many days hence.

As my hostess was talking the sun rose clear of the
eastern horizon, bathing the fields in dewy light. It was a scene
of awesome beauty, and moved me deeply; yet admiration
mingled strangely in my heart with sensations of pity and
horror, resultant on my landlady's revelations. 'This beautiful landscape, which appears with the freshness and untouched glory of Eden, is yet tainted by human evil,' I reflected. 'Nature nurses a viper in her bosom, a wilful and
vicious son at her breast. Oh, that Man could be wiped from
this earth!'

My thoughts reverted to Marianne - had she succeeded in overtaking that odious brute, Roland, and recap-
turing Belinda, without further hazard or mischance? Surely
the villain would let slip no opportunity to insult her afresh
- and she defenceless, unprotected.... Meanwhile my hostess was still talking, being clearly of a voluble disposition,
and before long, to my great astonishment, began to expound
on this very subject. She informed me that Marianne was now
safe, that - wonder of wonders! - Lord de L'Isle himself had
pursued Roland and recaptured Belinda, giving Roland a
large sum of money in exchange - further, that Marianne was

Lord de L'Isle's ward, and that he owned most of the land thereabouts. This was strange indeed!

'But is not Lord de L'Isle very young?' I ventured. 'If he is the gentleman who recently accosted me in my bedchamber - he seemed a mere stripling, in the very bloom of youth, the lightest of down upon his cheek ... '

'Nay - he looks young, I grant ye, but he is thirty. His parents died when he was just come of age, bequeathing him all their wealth, and a great castle on Sorrerby Rise; you may just glimpse its turrets, beyond that wood ... He travels much abroad, but in the intervals of his journeying, he has made great improvements to the estate and the village - building cottages for the poor and a new schoolhouse. Blessings on him! He is loved by all hereabouts, and deservedly so. 'Tis our dearest wish that he should marry, and produce an heir - otherwise, should he by some sad accident chance to die, the estate would fall by default to that villainous cousin of his, that Mr Roland Hooker Waller' - my hostess pronounced this name with a fine disdain.

'Mr Hooker Waller - the gentleman I crossed swords with, three nights past?'

'Aye, the very same, excepting he's no gentleman. 'Sewer rat' would be a more fitting description, for he's most vicious and corrupt - even to speak of him, it brings the bile swimming in my throat' - in eloquent proof of which, she spat on the cobbles.

'Is Mr Hooker Waller then universally disliked?'

'Aye, in these parts. He only hangs around here to cause mischief - otherwise he's mostly in London, gambling and frittering away his fortune - I should rather say, my Lord's fortune.'

'How!' I exclaimed. 'Is Lord de L'Isle then so blind to his cousin's faults - so easily deluded by him - so readily imposed upon? Does he bestow money freely upon this unworthy object - thus condoning, by implication, Mr Hooker Waller's debauched and vicious lifestyle?'

'I fear 'tis so,' she replied. 'Nothing is more mysterious, for Lord de L'Isle has as sharp and good a wit as any man, yet in this matter he appears befuddled and inconstant. Mr Hooker Waller comes and goes as he pleases, partaking frequently of Lord de L'Isle's hospitality - my lord keeps a fine cellar and the covers are laid each night, as befits his rank ... '

She continued talking thus, digressing proudly on the subject of my lord's wealth, nobility, condescension, and so on, but I heard no more; my head was in a whirl of new conceptions. So Mr Hooker Waller was a regular guest at the Castle - at Marianne's place of residence - and invited, nay even welcomed there by her so-called guardian, her supposed protector! What could be the meaning of this? Instantly I was filled with burning resolution - I must seek out Marianne and if possible rescue her from the dread castle, or at least offer her my service and protection - my heart, my sword, my life!

With this confirmed intent, I set out later that day, by foot, across the fields, and following the bank of a pleasant meandering river, soon arrived at the western boundary of Lord de L'Isle's estate. Here I paused - for the day was exceeding hot - to splash my face and dabble my feet in the clear running water. Impatient with constriction, I untied my bonnet and loosened my hair, so it tumbled free. Now truly I felt a daughter of Nature - like to some river naiad, or a dryad of the nearby woods. Sadly tanned and freckled, my hands roughened by country labour, I possessed nothing of Marianne's fair and ethereal beauty - yet my own body pleased me well enough. Sure, I would never wish to be a boy!

It was midday, and the sun having attained her zenith, the heat and glare were near insupportable. Instead of approaching the main gate of the Castle, therefore, I decided to walk through the woods, trusting to my luck and sense of direction, and hoping not to fall into any concealed mantraps. The beechwood was cool, well shaded and pleasant, though unexpectedly deep; an hour or so later, I was completely lost, and doubted my chances of emerging before nightfall.

It was then I heard voices nearby; familiar voices;

one low and well modulated, the other raised in sneering deprecation. Lord de L'Isle and Mr Hooker Waller! I crept forward, and before long found myself on the edge of a wide clearing.

The greensward was closely mown, and marble statues were disposed here and there, representations of goddesses and the heroines of classical mythology. In the centre stood Lord de L'Isle, a slim and upright figure, now dressed in satin small clothes and a coat of excellent tailoring, fitting tightly across the shoulders. As I perceived him, my heart seemed to miss a beat, or several, and my breath quickened, yet recollecting the brevity of our connection and the kindness he had hitherto shown me, I strove to calm myself. Surely I had no reason to fear the man - if I were discovered, it was unlikely he would do me any harm, or even reprove me for trespassing on his land. Mr Hooker Waller, at a few yards' distance, lounged indolently against a statue of Atlanta, smoking a cheroot.

'My dear cousin, pray cease to trouble yourself thus needlessly. I meant no harm to the girl, nor to that - one may scarce call it a horse - to that animal. I beg you will forget the whole disastrous episode - believe me, it is of very little significance.'

'Not to you, perhaps,' Lord de L'Isle replied, evenly. 'But you may recollect, Roland, that Marianne is my ward. Her parents being dead, I am now entrusted with her safekeeping - a duty which, believe me, I take seriously.'

'But how delightful for you. Mixing duty with pleasure, so to speak.'

'My task has so far proved the very opposite of delightful, or pleasurable. As you are well aware - and mainly due to your own interference -'

'My dear sweet coz, how can this be? I strive only to please you, in all things.'

'You would please me best by keeping your distance - by continuing to reside in London, as I think we agreed, and confining yourself to twice-yearly visits.'

'Ah yes, but then the air here is so invigorating, the

prospects so charming, and despite having a monthly income - your most generous settlement, dear coz - somehow I find myself continually short of money...'

'Due to foolish extravagance.'

'Possibly ...' Mr Hooker Waller finished his cheroot and threw it on the ground, grinding it with his heel.

'At all events, let me entreat you ...'

'Let us postpone your so-elegant entreaties to some future time; as you are aware, I dislike being lectured' - he took out a pocket watch - 'and I am engaged to be in London tomorrow night, so if you will excuse me' - and sweeping a low, mocking bow, he withdrew. I now perceived that the clearing formed the central meeting place of three wide and majestic avenues. Mr Hooker Waller sauntered away down the furthest of these, which I assumed led back to the house.

Left alone, Lord de L'Isle exhibited every sign of irritable exhaustion and despondency. He struck his forehead, and aimed several kicks at a statue of Venus reclining at her toilet; then sinking into a conveniently placed bench, of curious and ornate design, he rested his head despairingly in both hands, and moaned aloud.

It was scarcely possible to remain any longer in concealment. I could not thus stand by as witness to the distress and suffering of a fellow human being, without seeking in some way to alleviate it; and besides, I owed this particular gentleman a debt of kindness; so I walked forward. He remained unconscious of my presence till I was but a yard away; then a twig cracked, and he looked up in surprise. Recognition dawned in his eyes, followed swiftly by another expression, of glad interest.

'If I am disturbing you, my Lord, I crave your pardon, but I - I - ' My voice faltered and died.

'You are not,' he replied, gently. 'Pray sit down - I am happy to see you again, even at such a time as this. How much did you overhear of what just passed?'

'Hardly anything.' I sat down beside him, feeling confused and somewhat shy. He was so elegant! - unlike anybody I had ever known. His well manicured nails and long white fingers, his lightly powdered hair, the intricate fall of his necktie - all bespoke a gentleman of high breeding. Even his skin seemed to waft a faint perfume... How could I have anything in common with someone so infinitely civilized?

'Marianne is then your ward?' I ventured.

'Yes - and I owe you an apology, for my former behaviour. I was not quite open with you - for you see, I suspected you of being involved in my cousin's conspiracy.'

'How!' I exclaimed in astonishment, 'Me, conspiring with Mr Hooker Waller to abduct your ward?'

'Believe me, where Marianne is concerned, anything is possible - she attracts abductors, lovers, what you will, as a honey pot attracts flies. And do you then deny - did you never feel - ' His eyes held mine, and I felt the blood rise to my cheeks. 'Never mind,' he said, quickly. 'I will not question you.'

We sat for some while in silence. I perceived with dismay the full awkwardness of my position - for had it not indeed been my professed object in coming here to abduct Marianne, in the guise of a rescuer and supposedly in her interests? The arrows of self-accusation struck to my heart and remained there, quivering; I was o'erspread with shame's mantle.

My companion meanwhile had recommenced speaking, thanking me with sincerity for my protection of Marianne, and regretting my wound. Observing my confusion, he let the subject lapse and began instead to ply me with questions concerning my past life - where was my birthplace and what my parentage? I replied at first with hesitancy, but gradually gaining confidence, told him something of my mother and of Louisa.

He regarded me with wonder. 'And is it so?' he cried at last. 'Did these two women spend their lives together in happy and enduring love, faithful even unto the grave? And were these your parents?'

'My father died when I was a babe,' I replied. 'Louisa was my loving guardian, friend, sister and teacher; to my mother, all these and more, far more. They were happy indeed - and as for me, I should count myself fortunate to find a Friend of one tenth Louisa's worth.'

'I believe you,' he returned, warmly 'and I wish that I had known your stepmother, your guardian - she sounds a remarkable woman and an example to her Sex. I should have valued her acquaintance.'

'But she would scarcely have valued *yours*, for she greatly mistrusted and despised all *men*.' I spoke without thinking, and instantly regretting my words, wished that I had stayed silent - yet indeed, I had spoken nothing but truth.

He smiled faintly. 'And did she so? I have known other Ladies of that persuasion - friends of mine, whose judgement I approve entirely. Yet these Ladies, though despising my Sex in general, have made an exception for me.'

'Why so?'

'I cannot say. You will have to ask them. As it happens, they will be arriving here tonight, bringing a large party from London - they find my house a convenient place for dances and soirées. I could procure you an invitation, if you are willing to stay. I believe it is a coming out ball.'

While he was speaking, the sky had darkened rapidly, and soon huge drops of rain were falling here and there, in certain promise of a storm. We moved quickly to shelter, and taking my hand, he led me after him through the woods, until soon we came to a small roofed pavilion or summer-house, at a vantage point above the landscape.

It was a most glorious scene. From where we stood, the smooth green hillside swept down unhindered to a vast lake, which curved in serpentine fashion into the distance, giving the illusion of a winding river. In more clement, bright weather, I could imagine how the lake surface would glitter with a thousand sparkling lights; but now overhung by tumultuous grey clouds, it conveyed an awesome and sombre majesty. At some distance, I could see a foaming Cascade; near to it, the ruins of an Abbey; and on a far hillside, the entrance to what must be a network of underground Caves. Above all, I admired how clumps of trees stood here and there, most pleasing in their arrangement and drawing the eye towards distant prospects. The entire scene possessed all the splendour of an Italian painting; an effect unspoilt by the driving rain, now moving in sheets across the land.

'And did Nature do all this?' I exclaimed.

'She did little - although all was done in her Name,' replied Lord de L'Isle. 'The main part was contrived by Alice Brown, also known as Possibility Brown, a landscaper of consummate genius, though small fame - her brother takes all the credit for her work.

'And there is my house' - he pointed to the right. There at half a mile's distance against the grey sky I saw a huge castle with crenellated battlements, its every window blazing with light. A number of carriages were visible, drawn up outside the main gates.

'My guests have arrived,' he added. A smile crossed his lips, yet in his eyes lingered an indefinable expression of sadness. Watching him, I realized that despite his noble birth, his great wealth and fashionable friends, Lord de L'Isle was yet unhappy - even lonely. For a moment I glimpsed his true self, behind the mask. I wished to speak, yet dared not - and the next instant, he turned towards me.

As our eyes met, my heart seemed to dissolve into liquid silver, and for a moment I was near fainting. I could no longer deceive myself - I was stricken with dismay - surely it could not be that I loved a Man! Nothing in my upbringing had prepared me for such a horrible eventuality - it ran contrary to all my former inclinations and against all my most fervently held principles.

Turning aside, I strove to regulate my emotions and compose my features - happily, it was still raining, and my distress concealed, so I hoped, by the more general atmospheric turmoil.

At that moment, I heard the calling of a sweetly familiar voice, and Marianne appeared over the hill, in company with another Female - both were clad in voluminous riding capes, ample protection against the Elements. Marianne was leading a horse, whom by the simple plainness of her countenance and her cross-eyed squint, I assumed to be Belinda.

Marianne made exclamations of surprised pleasure on catching sight of me and saluted me on both cheeks, in sisterly fashion; I gladly returned the embrace. Meanwhile, the other female was shaking hands with Lord de L'Isle. She was a large woman, and in her manner and bearing, reminded me somewhat of Louisa, for though she wore no ornaments and was far from the ideal of female beauty - her greying hair was bound back severely, her nose a forbidding beak - yet she was obviously of high birth and accustomed to command. Soon she accosted me with a friendly air, made enquiry of my name and demanded an account of my past life and present journey; I answered her honestly, as seemed best.

While I was speaking, she and Lord de L'Isle exchanged several glances; and I thought he looked steadily at me, though I could not, for fear, meet his gaze.

'My dear,' she said at length, 'I am Melissa Cheverel. I knew your stepmother, Louisa, in her youth, and loved her well - indeed I may say that I owe everything to her good offices, for she encouraged and by example aided my Conversion, leading me to escape from the miserable constrictions of family and stultifying respectability. Through her I first encountered the author and foundation of all my present happiness, Amaryllis, to whom I will introduce you this evening. I assume you are coming to the Ball?'

I knew not how to reply, for though her kindness touched me and I was pleased to make her acquaintance, yet I was hardly in a mood for festivity. Besides, what would this great Lady think of me, when her clear gaze penetrated, as it surely would, the turmoil of my heart - when she discovered my perverted affection for Lord de L'Isle, which I could hardly yet admit even to myself? Surely she would turn from me in revolted scorn?

The rain lessening, our party began to descend the hillside. Belinda's pace was uneven, as she would often pause to crop the fresh verdure; so the others drew ahead, while Marianne, taking my arm, proceeded to discourse with animation on the superior wisdom of Animals. I attended with a heavy heart.

'Oh!' she exclaimed 'that human beings would only cultivate Natural Understanding - taking our example from such as my dear Horse. Our true needs are indeed very few and easily satisfied - principally for shelter and sustenance. Passionate love is a disorder of the natural emotions, resulting oftentimes in madness, and certainly antagonistic to Right Living. I am a subscriber to the New Philosophy of Mrs M. Humphry Allenby - if you are curious, I will gladly lend you her two most recent publications, the *Rediscovery of Happiness* and the *Return to Innocence*. Mrs Allenby's character is wholly admirable, and her writings would persuade even the - '

With a sudden access of spleen, I interrupted her. 'No doubt - but Marianne, whatever the extraordinary virtues of Mrs M. Humphry Allenby - whatever higher state this lady may happily have attained - you are still susceptible to passionate error; for but a few days past, I seem to recall, you consented foolishly to elope with Mr Hooker Waller. '

'No indeed! You are wholly mistaken on that score. Roland cunningly deluded me - I believed his intentions to be entirely honourable.'

'How! You thought he would offer marriage?'

'No - but he promised to accompany me to the horse fair at Mickleton Cross, which I had a great desire to see. Pray do not berate me - indeed, I deeply regret my naiveté on that occasion, especially as my dear guardian was forced to pay for it.'

Again we paused, for Belinda to savour an especially nourishing piece of vegetation. Lord de L'Isle and Miss Cheverel were now lost to view, having passed through the castle gates.

But why, I wondered, should Lord de L'Isle have given money to Mr Hooker Waller - wherefore such craven behaviour towards a traitorous and despicable villain? Was this not strange? I expressed my bewilderment to Marianne, and she flushed.

'My guardian has a - a secret, which I am not at liberty to reveal. It explains All - and yet for his own safety, it must remain closely guarded. Perhaps if you ask him - I note he has a fondness for you ...'

My heart gave a lurch. A fondness! Yes, he was fond of me - no more than fond. As for love - no. Perhaps he loved Marianne - or perhaps Mr Hooker Waller! Yes, that was surely the explanation: Mr Hooker Waller had spurned Lord de L'Isle's advances and was now blackmailing him, threatening to reveal his secret passion to the world! My mind moved with a marvellous rapidity, building conjecture upon conjecture. Thus engaged, to the exclusion of all else, I took absent-minded leave of Marianne in the stable courtyard and wandered into the great entrance hall of the castle.

All around was bustle and movement - here a chambermaid scurried past carrying a pile of bed linen, and another with silver branched candlesticks; there two cooks, in animated discussion; and here a deputation of gardeners, bringing baskets of earthy vegetables and orchard fruits. All were women - a peculiarity that failed to strike me at the time, for I was admiring the vastness of the hall, with its flagstoned floor and huge pillars soaring to a fan-vaulted ceiling.

The housekeeper came forward, seemingly unsurprised by my arrival, and welcomed me kindly, introducing herself as Mrs Weston. She led me up a broad red-carpeted staircase and along a corridor hung with portraits; then, selecting a key from the bundle at her waist, she unlocked a door and opened it.

On entering the chamber, I exclaimed aloud with delight; for besides being nobly furnished, with a majestic four poster bed and ornately framed pictures and looking glasses on the walls, it was decked throughout with the most beautiful flowers. They were principally roses - roses of the deepest red and the purest white, and of heavenly scent. As I stood captivated, several chambermaids entered, carrying jugs of steaming hot water, which they poured into a tub, standing on three feet fashioned like animal paws.

Mrs Weston turned to me. 'My Lord gave instructions, Miss, that you would need dry stockings and shoes and a gown for tonight's ball. Everything is provided here, as you will find ... ' She unlocked the closet and left it a little ajar, then curtseyed and withdrew.

All was peaceful, save for occasional sounds of laughter, and women's voices below the windows: Lord de L'Isle's guests, I presumed, now taking exercise in the gardens, following the passing of the storm. Glancing down, I saw my garments were sodden with rain and liberally splashed with mud. I undid my gown and stepped out of it; then thought it best to uncover my long-forgotten wound, which proved to be near healed.

Curious to view my reflection, I walked forward to the nearest glass; and to my surprise, found that I looked almost beautiful. My eyes, darker and more open, my parted lips, the burning summer in my cheeks - all betrayed what I would fain conceal.

In the ensuing silence, I heard a rose drop her velvet petals, one by one; some fell on the carpet, and others into my bath water, where they floated and idly drifted.

I bathed with pleasure, and emerged from the water in good spirits.

Opening the closet, I found a dress of yellow silk and brocade, heavy and richly patterned, with a hooped petticoat and another of silver lace. Ranged on a shelf below were a great many shoes - I liked best a pair of yellow satin, which happily fitted me exactly. Rejecting a fan of painted chicken skin with ivory sticks, I picked another of gilded paper.

The day was fading and a maid entered carrying a taper, to light the candles in my room. She was very young and herself appeared surrounded by a soft radiance of golden light - it seemed she might have kindled the candles just with her fingertips. She stayed to help me with my hair, and from time to time gave a gentle sigh.

'What ails you?' I demanded. She made no answer, but her eyes, meeting mine in the glass, told all. Love is indeed the finest melancholy, spilling over in sighs and tears. 'Will you meet her tonight?' I asked.

She nodded. 'But first I must light all the candles, and help the ladies to dress...'

I took the comb from her hand and pushed her towards the door. 'Go now,' I said. 'Leave your taper; I shall light the candles. The ladies can dress themselves, I daresay.'

Instruments were being tuned below and would occasionally break into a waltz or quadrille. I felt a growing excitement. This would be my first ball! - and perhaps if I drank enough negus or ratafie, I might put Lord de L'Isle from my thoughts and find my affections turning towards a more suitable object.

I went down the corridor, knocking and entering at every door. Some of the bedchambers were empty; in others I encountered a lady at her toilet, or several of them together, laughing and talking. I received some curious glances, but lit the candles and was gone before any could question me.

Having crossed the stairwell, I came to an oaken door of imposing dimensions. I tried the handle; it opened easily and I entered, carrying my taper before me.

The room was huge and made sombre by the deepening dusk. I could descry a bay window at the far end, and bookcases lining the two long walls and reaching to the ceiling - itself an impressive specimen of ornate plasterwork. I walked forward incautiously, prompted by my desire to examine the books; nearest were a number of bound calfskin volumes of Shakespeare's plays and the collected works of Mr Pope; but I got no further, for a shadowy figure moved with heart-stopping suddenness from an alcove and strong fingers closed around my wrist. I gasped for fright and nearly dropped the taper - but he took it from me in time. It was Lord de L'Isle!

Keeping his eyes steady upon mine, he moved back a pace; then turned to light a branch of candles, standing in a niche. Our shadows danced and stretched up to the ceiling like giants.

He was dressed in grey satin with old lace at his wrists and throat, a light dress sword fastened by his side, and broad diamond buckles on his shoes.

'Did you hope to avoid me?' he said, lightly.

'I - I - no,' I stammered. 'I had no such desire - I am honoured to be your guest.'

'Yet your expression indicates a certain displeasure. Pray tell me, have I disgusted you in any way - or insulted you?'

'No - no - '

'Then why ...?'

The blood rose to my face in a burning tide. My wrist still ached sorely from his clasp and I rubbed at it with a sense of grievance - it would very likely bruise. In sudden anger, I exclaimed, 'I need not tell you my thoughts - you have no right to cross-examine me thus. You keep your own secrets - then let me keep mine!'

A window was opened beneath. Sweet strains of music floated out on the evening air, and then a woman's voice singing:

> 'Whoe'er she be
> That not impossible She
> That shall command my heart and me;
>
> Where'er she lie,
> Lock'd up from mortal eye
> In shady leaves of destiny:
>
> - Meet you her, my Wishes
> Bespeak her to my blisses,
> And be ye call'd, my absent kisses ... '

Feeling a little giddy headed, I sank into the window seat. 'Have you eaten?' he enquired.

'Not since this morning ...'

'There is a cold collation laid out below - but if we are to exchange heart's confidences, it had best not be in a crowded ballroom. Besides, your descent is eagerly awaited - I would scarce have you to myself a moment. Let me order a tray to be brought up.' He tugged the bellpull. 'By the way, you know it is a masked ball this evening. I have always been greatly interested in masks. When I was young, I spent a year in Venice, where the mask-makers ply their trade, by the Bridge of Sighs. Of these the most famous was Bartolomeo de San Servino, who had begun his career by casting the death masks of great noblemen and poets. His masks were so like real faces, you would believe they smiled sometimes, or grew melancholy. I saw a mask he made of the moon, that was said to confer immortality upon its owner: but you would have to accustom yourself to waxing and waning. One young married lady of my acquaintance sold her beautiful pearl ring and her emerald brooch to buy his mask of a female wolf. She was advised not to wear this until after her pregnancy was past, but the carnivale falling in her sixth month, she could not resist - the results were exactly as predicted. Her husband ordered the child to be drowned. As for me, I was twenty-one, my parents had just died, I was unable to sleep at nights. When I entered the mask shop, Bartolomeo himself came forward to the counter: he looked not more than twenty, though I believe in that year he was 102. He refused to serve me, informing me that it was not advisable to place one mask on top of another. "That you wear" he said, pointing in my face "is already in a way to killing you."'

In the next week, made bold by terror, I revealed my secret to a number of friends; then I felt the mask loosen its grip; I gained a little breathing space. Otherwise, I do believe it would have suffocated me. For you see, it is one of those dead men's faces .... I had a twin brother and he was the heir to my parents' estate; when we were ten years old and my mother past childbearing age, he died. Anxious to secure the succession - for the estate, like most, was entailed in favour of a male heir - they determined that I should be a boy - that I should be, in effect, my brother. So they gave it out, 'twas the girl that died. And now, since I have told you my secret, can you trust me with yours?'

Mrs Weston had answered the bell, and brought us a number of little dishes on a tray, and gone away again, before I was anywhere near speaking.

'And Mr Hooker Waller?' I managed at last. 'Is he aware of - of what you have just told me?'

'If he were, the whole of Society would also know it within a day or two, and Roland would be installed in his rightful place, as Master of this estate. He would be Lord de L'Isle - and I, plain Cordelia Beaufort. He senses his power over me, nonetheless, and makes use of it. I expect he will find out eventually - then I shall be forced to flee the country and live abroad - the estate will go to rack and ruin under his ownership, for he would care naught, either for the land or for its people. You may well think me an unsuitable protector for Marianne - possessing a borrowed past and no future, living ever in the uncertain present - but at least I provide a home for her. Her parents entrusted her to me, knowing all. If you love her indeed, I give you leave to hazard your suit, though you have not much chance of success, I warn you - others have tried - '

I stood up, though doubting the strength of my legs, but apprehending that I must speak now, seizing the opportune moment, and disperse all lingering clouds of doubt and illusion. 'I would make a poor suitor in truth, for my heart is already given away. I love you, Cordelia! - and consequent upon your most welcome revelation, my Will and my Reason now join with my Heart, in preferring you above all others. If you will not have me, I must - I must - ' I was meaning to say, I must depart, and glanced uncertainly towards the door, but at that instant, she seized me in her arms and kissed me!

Oh! - the joy that flooded my heart! - I had never imagined, never allowed myself to conceive such happiness! It seemed natural and easy to return her embraces - though having the advantage of me in height and strength, she pressed me to her so hard I could scarce breathe and was soon forced to entreat her for a moment's respite. As she released me, I saw that her eyes were shining and her cheeks flushed - all bitterness and cynicism vanished from her countenance - no longer the sad young man, but a woman of great beauty and noble demeanor. Our lips met again, this time with tender hesitancy.

'Oh Abby,' she breathed, 'stay with me, be mine - I will love you forever!' Taking my hand, she covered it with kisses.

'Yes dearest, for a lifetime and more. We must never again be parted, I could not endure it. As to where we live,' I added, 'it hardly matters - this castle is wholly delightful, but indeed I would welcome the opportunity of foreign travel.'

Our conversation continued a good while longer, mixed with a thousand caresses and sweet endearments, which having pity on my reader, I forbear to describe. At eleven o'clock, with exceeding reluctance, we descended to the ballroom, where Melissa welcomed us with composure and the merest flicker of a raised eyebrow. I was introduced to stately Amaryllis, Duchess of —, and a great number of other ladies, including several of the old nobility, others of scholarly renown or possessed of great artistic genius, and many fresh in the bloom and gaiety of youth. Having never before seen ladies dancing together, or paying such open tribute of sisterly kindness and affection, I revelled in the Spectacle; it recalled to me the poet's words:

'There all the happy souls that ever were,
Shall meet with gladness in one theatre;
And each shall know, there, one another's face,
By beatific virtue of the place ....'

The central embellishment of the long refreshment table was an Ice Bowl, filled with chopped fruits; a device of marvellous conception and cunning execution; for though composed of frozen water it did not melt, only its frosty surface after several hours turned clear and glistened; and sweet pea flowers hung suspended therein, as if growing in air. This appeared to me an emblem of the heart: she who desires love must be content to wait in patience for her reward; break the bowl before it melts and you would tear and destroy the flowers - and so on.

I had almost forgot to say, Mr Hooker Waller came to a violent end - for having stayed late and drunk deep that night in the village tavern, and falling in with a pack of dastardly ruffians, and attempting in their company to rob a gentleman's carriage, he was first shot and then crushed by a rock. So all ends happily.

ACDC

TARA RIMSK

'It's all a bit confused.'

'Do you want to tell me about it?'

'Thanks, Di, but I think we'd better order first if we've only got an hour. Can you see what today's specials are?'

I made a rapid choice as did Di, she risking a glass of red wine, me opting for perrier water.

'You see, it all started when I met A.'

'A?' repeated Di, sounding slightly mystified.

'Yes - look it's clearer if I speak in initials,' I hissed, glancing meaningfully at the adjacent table where a bellicose business man sat studying the menu.

'So what happened when you met A?' asked Di, lowering her voice.

'Well, I was immediately attracted by her, entranced actually. One glance from those sloe-black eyes and I felt like a tub of stork margarine melting in the sun.'

'Gosh,' responded Di sympathetically. 'It must have been quite something!'

'Yes, but there was always an elusive quality about her. I never felt she could be truly mine. She was like an exquisite butterfly floating up and down my arteries but never quite settling in my heart.'

Di pensively loosened a strand of truant spaghetti from her fork back on to her plate.

'So A never made it into either ventricle?'

'Exactly, and this was just as well, for it wasn't long

before I discovered she was much more seriously involved with B.'

'Ah,' exclaimed Di, rotating a more compliant strand of pasta. 'So she was flirting with you while sleeping with another! Women!'

We sighed, as women of the world do on such occasions, and I noticed the bellicose business man shoot us a curious look as he tucked a large pink serviette into his shirt collar.

'I must say this fettucini al salmone is delicious,' said I loudly, attempting to make our conversation sound less intriguing.

'Anyway, while I was recovering from a bruised aorta, I myself met someone else - someone older and more mature, who was - probably still is - a social worker.'

'C?' enquired Di sagely.

'No, we won't give her an initial since she doesn't come into the story that much. It would only confuse things. By now I could observe A and B together with equanimity. I was even able to appreciate how well the firm and solid-looking B complemented the light and flippant A. Being involved in an affair of my own had done wonders for my powers of detachment as far as A was concerned.

'An affair of my own,' murmured Di; 'rather a lovely phrase - a bit like "a room of one's own" ...'

'But a damned sight harder to find,' I retorted, inexplicably irritated by Di's dreamy tones. 'Anyway, to cut a long story short, A began to talk of visiting Australia, where several of her relatives now lived. No one took this very seriously. A was full of bright ideas she never actually executed. I was not the only one who found it difficult to imagine her in a sheep and shears context.'

'No,' laughed Di, 'she doesn't sound exactly cut out for the society of bovid mammals.'

I shot Di a sharp look. Was she mocking me? Her eyelids were demurely lowered as she sipped her chianti classico.

'One evening I went to a cafe with my old friend C and we met up with A and B. It was one of those fine summer evenings when the litter on the streets gleams incandescent under a Camden sunset, and even the tramps by the tube station seem transfigured.'

'Go on, go on!' murmured Di, 'I can just see it.'

(We were both drinking red wine by now.)

'You know how sensitive I am, Di; well, the sight of that full orb setting over Camden High Street had triggered off all kinds of emotion. And I sat in the cafe, overcome by melancholia, nostalgia, neuralgia and ....'

'Did the others notice?' Di asked alarmed.

'They had little choice but to notice, for suddenly I began to tell them the story of my life.'

'Oh no!' Di looked distinctly nauseous.

'What's the matter? Does sphaghetti al pesto disagree with you? Anyway, I told them about my first love which had lasted for nearly ten years.'

'You told them about each year?'

'I did, Di. I felt like a woman possessed. I had to speak. Finally, after about three or four hours, I came to an abrupt halt. A was asleep, her curly black hair falling over the table. It dawned on me then that she'd never shown any real interest in my life. C was staring out of the window as she spooned the froth off her capuccino. She'd heard the whole story several times before. But B - B was looking at me with all the intensity of someone experiencing a divine revelation. Our eyes met over the sugar bowl and I felt like ....'

'A tub of Stork margarine,' interjected Di triumphantly.

'No, Di.' I shook my head with annoyance at her coarseness. 'I felt as if I were a pound of Lurpak butter basking in the sun!'

'How romantic, but -'

'But what Di?'

'Surely the butter would melt rather than bask, wouldn't it?'

'I know it would. That's the whole point! The heart does melt; it basks and it melts - like margarine, like butter, both ...'

'Both, we 'ave both if you want them, Signora,' said the waiter anxiously. 'You want butter on its own - 'is not good. Better with bread.'

'Oh, I'm sorry. No, we don't want any bread or butter, thank you. Could you bring us the menu again please!'

I looked across at Di. She was shaking with suppressed laughter. The man at the adjacent table was slowly unwrapping a parcel of silver foil and depositing the contents on to his plate.

'But Tara,' said Di, suddenly serious; 'do you mean to say that your mature social worker lover no longer had the power to reduce you even to butterfat?'

'How intuitive you are, Di! Yes, I can't help but feel that my involvement with her was inextricably linked to my rejection by the flirtatious A. But before you accuse me of having merely been on the rebound, you should know that my lover was in a parallel situation. She had just split up with someone, so we were looking to each other to provide a haven from past storms.'

'And do I detect that this mutual haven was beginning to turn into a trap?'

'That's exactly it, Di! By now she was looking back over her shoulder towards her former lover - at least I sensed that's what she was doing; and I - by implication - was free to respond to B.'

'Except that B wasn't free to respond to you.'

'Ah, but this is where the plot thickens. A started making concrete plans to go to Australia and B - to my amazement and delight - began to flirt outrageously with me.'

'But how did you and B manage to see each other alone?' asked Di in dubious tones.

'We didn't! I never saw her away from A and so had no way of finding out what her behaviour to me implied - if indeed it implied anything at all.'

Di frowned into her empty glass.

I tried to catch the waiter's attention by giving a series of commanding nods and conspiratorial winks. These served only to distract the businessman opposite, who ladled a forkful of sphaghetti al vongole into his serviette instead of his mouth. Both Di and I watched fascinated as two tiny mussels dripping with tomato sauce slowly crept on to his paunch, there to reside.

'Yes, can we have two glasses of house red please!'

'Certe, Signora.' The waiter smiled at us and shook his head sadly in the direction of the businessman's belly.

'Go on,' said Di; 'What happened then?'

'Well, C invited B and me to go on holiday with her and a couple of male friends. I accepted with alacrity as did B. My heart gave a sudden leap. A was due to fly to Australia just before Christmas. The rest of us were to spend Christmas with our respective families and then drive down to Cornwall for the New Year.

'As December approached. I felt as if I were in the grip of a high fever. I ate without noticing what I ate and even woke early in the mornings - an almost unprecedented state of affairs with me. I still saw A and B together, usually in the company of C, but the strain of constantly having to conceal my feelings for B was taking its toll. I contracted flu and took the week off work. I was too depressed to do anything other than reread *The Well of Loneliness* and listen to Leonard Cohen.'

'Some cure!' laughed Di.

'There was one particular evening when I felt I had reached my nadir. I was listening to *So Long Mariannne* and wondering whether my feet were large enough to earn me the title of invert, when the phone rang. It was late, about 11.30 pm, when I idly stretched out for the receiver ....

' "Hallo there, it's me," said A.

' "Hi," I replied, trying to summon up an impression of cheeriness. It was a long time since she and I had talked on our own together. After a strained exchange of pleasantries, she suddenly said: "So, do you have anything to confess now I'm going away?"

'The lightness of her tone did not deceive me. I could hear my heart thumping against my chest. If she had but known it, A came closer at that moment to the very ventricles than ever before.

' "I don't know where I stand with you anymore," continued the voice, half-angry, half-pleading.

' "I can understand how you must be feeling," I replied in what I hoped were soothing tones.

' "Oh, you can, can you? I very much doubt that." A was openly hostile now. "What kind of a friend are you, Tara? B and I have been going through some difficult times recently and this has not been helped by your sudden intense interest in B!"

'I didn't dare reply that my sudden interest in B had a lot to do with B's sudden interest in me. A confrontation of this kind was the last thing I wanted. Since B had never openly declared her feelings for me, I knew I stood on shifting sands. I blew my nose loudly and coughed into the receiver.

'"Are you crying?" asked A, a trifle too sharply.

'"No, A, I've got a cold, it's late and I'm going to bed. Goodnight," and I put the phone down before she had a chance to reply.

'Questions pierced me like sharp arrows as I tossed and turned in bed that night. Was A leaving B for a short break or forever? What did she mean by "difficult times" with B? And where, oh where, was B in all this?

'When I finally fell into a fitful sleep, I dreamed that A and I were climbing some ancient ruins on a cliff top - it could have been Tintagel. Far below us B was climbing down some endless steps (so it must have been Tintagel). A was watching me watching B and suddenly she called out in a sing-song voice;

"You can't play with B
You can't play with B
You can only play with me"

'The malevolent little nursery rhyme rang in my head all the next day.'

'Thank God!' exclaimed Di, raising her glass to her lips.

'For what?' I queried surprised by the vehemence of her tone.

'Thank God my life's not like yours!'

'Well, thanks. Are you bored? Would you rather talk about something else?'

'Oh no - sorry Tara - I didn't mean it like that! Please go on. Tell me what happened when you went to Cornwall.'

No less than three pleading glances from Di finally inspired me to resume my tale.

'Ah Cornwall - yes - I can remember it all so clearly. We stayed in a huge old house which belonged to C's family. It was right on the coast at Bedruthan Steps.'

'Bed, Rough and what ...?' exclaimed Di.

'Bedruthan Steps,' I repeated, ignoring my companion's crude attempts at humour.

'The wind howled day and night outside our bedrooms like a demented banshee, while the five of us huddled over wine and whisky in the drawing room. The fire place had been blocked up long ago, so we were forced to imbibe spirits as our only access to warmth. No one had set foot in the place since C's grandmother had died of a heart attack, and the air was dank and musty, as if the gloved hand of death yet rested on the oak banisters.

'I can still see C uncorking a bottle of Beaujolais Nouveau from the local offie - her pale eyes slightly glazed from the excesses of the previous evening, and B - B with her corn blonde hair and green green eyes throwing back her head and laughing at me in that warm, teasing way....'

'Excuse me. You 'ave chosen?'

'Er, no - Di, what would you like?'

'I'm not sure. What's Tirami Su?'

'I will describe,' exclaimed our waiter joyfully. '...Is like a soft sponge soaked in spirit with vanilla pod and - 'ow you say? - a custard melting in chocolate all floating in ....'

'Enough!' I cried, moved almost to tears by this exquisite vision, appearing as it did when I was submerged in the sour crabapple jelly of memory.

Di saw the tears swelling in my eyes and interjected with, 'We'll have two Tirami Sus swimming in whatever.'

The waiter looked highly satisfied by our response and I overheard him saying to the waitress as he passed her: 'Is not true what they say about the English reserve. The two signoras in the corner have tears in their eyes when I describe Tirami Su.'

'Where did I get to, Di?'

'You were talking about B.'

'Oh yes. Well, I'd already confided in C about my feelings for B, which were of course inflamed by our being in such close proximity. On that first evening C and I talked further in her bedroom once the others had retired. The lamp had fused, so we had to light candles. They cast green shadows on the walls, surrounding us in an unholy glow. C was a good listener and cautioned my impatient spirit.

'"Beware," she said: "I've talked to B on her own many times and it seems to me that she's still infatuated with A."

'"How can she be?" I retorted angrily. "When it's obvious that A is nothing but a gaudy butterfly. How many staunch Australian women with tanned, surf-swept bodies is she seducing even as we speak?"

'"I don't know," said C, and we both sighed.

'The whisky was finished and rain pounded against

the dilapidated sash window. I took a candle in my hand and stumbled up the first flight of stairs, pausing for a moment outside B's door. There was no sound. Was she fast asleep, dreaming of ...? A sudden cough brought me back to earth. B smoked about fifty a day and I often wondered how she looked so fresh and healthy in the circumstances. Emboldened by whisky I toyed with the idea of knocking on her door on the pretext of offering her an ashtray. But in the end I forced myself to carry on up the creaking stairs until I reached the attic.'

'*Due Tirami Su per due belle donne!*' announced our waiter grandly.

They did indeed look magnificent, and there was a reverential silence while Di and I munched our way through the layers of spirited sponge and floating chocolate custard.

Suddenly Di looked up at me with tears in her eyes.

'What's wrong?' I asked, momentarily distracted from my 'fragments d'un discours amoureux'. 'Are you too moved by the Tirami Su?'

'Yes,' said Di, tears meandering down her flushed cheeks. 'You know what you said about the sour crabapple jelly of memory ... you're so right!'

'Di, one day you must tell me the story of your life,' said I kindly before returning to my own 'histoire'.

'That night I could not sleep but writhed and squirmed as one flung upon a stormy sea or a soft mattress. Just as I was about to drift off, a growl of thunder brought me again to my wretched senses. I got up and went to the window. The air was thick with cloud, blocking out my usual view of the sea below. The moon was a pale slither of gouda gliding through the mist. Suddenly lightning struck the window ledge, flooding the whole attic with icy light. I fled back to my bed and, out of fear rather than cowardice, pulled the blankets over my head and curled up in the foetal position.

'Unfortunately, inability to breathe forced me to fling back the bedclothes. I opened my eyes to see a shadow on the wall, a green shadow, staring down at me.'

'You mean it had a face?' gasped Di, clutching her glass.

'I do indeed, Di. You can imagine how shocked I was. I closed my eyes and tried to block it out but it spoke to me.'

'What did it say?'

'It said: "I am the ghost of C's grandmother, and from time to time I like to visit my old bedroom."'

'When I forced myself to look at her again, I could clearly make out a woman's shape projected on the wall like a hologram. Two eyes fringed with long green eyelashes blinked at me.'

'Tara,' said Di solemnly, 'you don't think that the whisky...?'

'You want whisky too, signora?' enquired our waiter, depositing a glass of the lethal liquid on the businessman's table.

'No - just two coffees please. Di, do you want an expresso? Yes - two expressos, thank you.'

'...'Is a pleasure, signora. You enjoyed Tirami Su?'

'Oh yes,' replied Di, 'It was an experience beyond compare.'

She was awarded a beatific beam for this last remark.

'So what else did C's grandmother say besides the fact she liked to revisit old haunts?'

'She told me to have courage and reach out with both hands for what I wanted. She said she'd brought up C's mother to do that, and C's mother had done the same with C - and look what happy and well-balanced people they were.'

'Did she imply you weren't?'

'She said I was an ultra-sensitive spirit who hadn't yet learnt to manipulate fate. Then she went on at length about determinism and free will and something about Hobbs and peaches. Stuff like that. I wasn't really listening.'

Di looked disappointed. She had a PhD in philosophy.

'Anyway, the upshot was that she made a sort of prediction designed to help me out since I appeared to be incapable of helping myself. She decreed that the next day we would go on a coastal walk from Port Quinn to Port Isaac. I was to wait until we reached the highest point between the two ports and there I was to accost B and find out once and for all the meaning of her flirtatiousness towards me. "It's your last chance," she said, "before the year is out." Then she disappeared.'

'Gosh!' said Di, 'I bet that put an end to your night's sleep!'

'No, just the opposite. I slept like a log after that and woke up feeling strong and resolved.'

'So did you follow the ghost's advice?'

'I'm coming to that. I went down to breakfast at about 10.00 am. B and C were already tucking into toast and home-made marmalade. Only the two boys slept on. B said: "Well, where shall we go for our final walk this year?"

'C replied, "Let's do the walk from Port Quinn to Port Isaac. It's by far the most dramatic stretch of coast."

'"Is that okay by you, honey?" B was addressing me, her arm outstretched in a lazy gesture.

'"Yes, sure," I said weakly and rose to put on my trainers.

'"Tell the boys to get a move on," called B. "We haven't got all day." '

'An hour or so later the five of us disembarked at Port Quinn. The sea was wild and foam soared upwards like flocks of white doves seeking refuge.'

'How beautiful!' exclaimed Di soulfully.

'Yes, normally I would have climbed slowly, pausing to assimilate each view and perhaps pen a sonnet on the passing waves. But of course I had to make sure I reached the highest point of the walk at the same time as B.'

'Did you say B was taller than you?'

'That was the problem. B strode ahead, oblivious of

my plight and able to cover huge stretches of ground with seemingly no effort. C was also taller than me and so kept pace with B more easily. The lads were dawdling deliberately and giggling together.'

'Were they in a couple?'

'No, they were just buddies who enjoyed discussing each other's boyfriends.'

'So what did you do?'

'I carried on walking between the two groups. Whenever I was fairly sure B and C wouldn't turn round to admire the view, I scampered surreptitiously up a slope, but of course my main aim was to look calm and composed by the time I reached the highest point. I couldn't risk running too much and being completely out of breath at the crucial moment, so I had to resort to a ploy:

'"Help!" I cried loudly, "I think I've sprained my ankle."

'They didn't hear the first time and I felt rather silly having to repeat myself but it worked. B came charging down the cliff at full speed, her blonde hair shimmering in the pale winter sun.

'"Lean on me," she said in that deep, husky voice, and slowly, we ascended the cliff together, me trying to remember which ankle was supposed to be sprained.

'The thrill of feeling her arm round my waist made me feel almost weightless, as if we could float to the top of the cliff effortlessly like wind-borne seagulls.'

'How romantic!' sighed Di, staring into her empty coffee cup.

'At last, the time had come. C was miles ahead and the boys miles behind. I took my courage in both hands.

'"B, it's the last day of the year and I have to speak. What kind of game are you playing?"

'"I beg your pardon."

'"Don't pretend not to understand. Just tell me what sort of game you're playing with A and me."

"'I don't play games," retorted B, flashing me a smile so ravishing I felt myself dissolving into thin air. I tried to keep my voice as measured and mellifluous as was compatible with high blood pressure and a palpitating heart.

"'What the hell did you mean - flirting with me in front of A as you did before she went away? It didn't go unnoticed you know! A even attacked me over it. I can only assume that you enjoy causing pain. Are you some kind of sadist or what ...?"

'I was aware that my voice was emerging as a hoarse shriek, not dissimilar to the kind of sound which might be produced by a seagull with a hangover.

'Tears stung my cheeks and I moved away from B and tried to look impassive, as if my face were wet with sea foam only.

"'Hey, honey, don't cry!" said B, all sympathy, pursuing me along the cliff path.

"'How dare you call me honey! You don't give a damn about me!" I was moving fast now - sprained ankle quite forgotten - as I began to scale a rock which jutted out over the sea.

"'Tara, come back! Can't you see the notice - it's dangerous - crumbling cliff!"

"'What does that matter? You don't care if I live or die, so why should I?"

'Never had I felt so bold. The wind and salt lashed my cheeks, mingling with the tears which constantly blocked my vision. I climbed with unaccustomed fluency along a narrow track and finally reached a boulder precariously balancing on a few flat rocks. I flung myself down and gave way to a wild burst of weeping.

'After a few seconds I felt B's arm round me, dragging me back from the edge.

"'Darling," I murmured into her jacket sleeve.

'She took out an extra large mens' handkerchief (I think it was a Liberty's design) and I blew my nose into it several times.

"'Tara,'" she said - and the gentleness of her tone almost made me swoon. "Listen, honey, I think you should know that my affair with A is completely over, whether or not she returns from Australia."

'A small speck of hope crept into my heart and nestled there like a baby bird.

"'Oh B...,'" I murmured, pressing myself closer against her.

"'I never meant to hurt you, Tara!'"

"'I know, I know,'" I whispered consolingly; "It doesn't matter now!"

"'But,'" continued B; "can't you see I'm having an affair with C!'"

Di gasped, 'Oh Tara!'

The sight of her sympathetic face across the table brought tears to my eyes, and I wept copiously into my serviette. By now Di was crying too. I thought wistfully of B's Liberty handkerchief returned to her the moment we got back from Cornwall, though I'd had the good grace to wash it first. Mercifully our sobbing was half concealed by the music. In my agitated, freshly depressed state, the lyrics struck me with fresh poignancy:

> *Don't tell me to stop crying*
> *please just hold me while I do*
> *Soothe me with your silence and just cradle me to you*
> *Don't push me for my reasons or expect me to explain*
> *How can I in five minutes shift*
> *a lifetime's hidden pain?*

Through a veil of tears I saw a tray looming towards us on which perched two liqueur glasses spurting small flames.

'Signore, sambucca - compliments of the house! I cannot bear to see due belle donne so un'appy. Tell your boyfriends they should look after you better than this or you find new friends! You tell them this from me! Please - accept!'

Di and I nodded as graciously as possible with our

noses wrapped in our serviettes. The waiter gingerly picked up the businessman's pink serviette - now ornately garnished with crushed mussels - and rather less gingerly, pocketed the tip. Neither Di nor I had even noticed our bellicose neighbour leave.

We sipped the flaming sambucca in silence, still haunted by the plaintive voice of Julia Fordham:

> Don't tell your girlfriend about me
> 'cos your girlfriend
> Won't like girls like me
> Don't tell your girlfriend about me
> If you just hold me, hold me, hold me.

'How could she?' cried Di with sudden vehemence.

'Who in particular?' I enquired, still snivelling into my sambucca.

'Oh - I don't know! How could A do that to B and B and C do that to you?'

'I don't know either. Why do people do these things to each other?'

Di threw me a searching look across the table.

'Have you ever thought ...' She spoke so softly I could hardly hear her, 'Have you ever thought of taking an interest in another letter of the alphabet - D - for example?'

I returned her gaze until I felt myself drowning in the mauve radiance of her eyes.

'Di,' I whispered, as we stared deep into each other's orbs, 'Di, I never noticed this before, but your eyes are the colour of crocuses ....'

My voice trailed away with emotion. On the tablecloth the folded bill lay poised between us like a giant question mark.

THE GREEN GRASS OF WYOMING

CHRISTINA DUNHILL

I always wanted to live with horses. That was what kept me going when I was a kid. Me and Tina sharing one small room while our brother, mad Mikey, had the loft to himself. And boys all around outside, messing up the neighborhood, hanging out on the corners or draping themselves over fire escapes. People said I had an attitude. It started when Harry Salzer lifted up my skirt from behind when I was taking a drink at the fountain. I just waited for him to take his turn, then smashed his head against the nozzle; he came up with his mouth bleeding and went straight to Mrs Weingarten.

'Boys can't help being curious,' said Mrs Weingarten to me.

'Does that mean boys don't have brains, Ma'am?' I said, 'I'd be real curious to open his head up and take a look.'

'You better get a grip on yourself, young lady, said Mrs Weingarten, you have an attitude.'

Yes, I thought, and it's going to stay that way.

No room at home. Everywhere I went I had to take my kid sister: school, girl scouts, grocery store, drug store. I dreamed of two things: space and isolation. I wanted the prairies, I wanted the plains. Anywhere away from the Lower East Side. The dirt and noise and height of it. And the boys. Sometimes I'd even envy the Polish girls whose mothers made them stay in. I wished Mom saw me as a precious gift to be preserved for someone. No chance. Mom saw me as more hands round the house and a chaperone for Tina and golden boy. I'd lock myself in the bathroom sometimes and read horse stories. *Indian Paint* was my favourite. This young 'Indian' boy, they called him, tames a wild piebald colt and rides it to peaks of daring none of the grown braves comes near. He rides it bareback, guiding it with his knees only and a little pressure one side or other of its neck. This pony has never known the misery of a bit between the teeth and sometimes he makes his own way, galloping across the plains to the secret places he shows the boy, fast as the wind with his young rider clinging on as best he can. The boy and the pony are in love, no doubt of that. They live for each other.

Mind you, it had gotten me a few scars, this behavior. Mom would come banging on the bathroom door. Once she broke it down when I wouldn't open up. Once she hit me for laying into mad Mikey when he started to rib me for being an egghead. We didn't read books in my family. And there was the time she'd tried to throw a whole bunch of forks and knives at me to lay the table and got confused and threw the pan of rice instead, boiling water and all. The scar from that goes all down the right side of my neck and shoulder. But I still have a face like a baby. All the girls say that. How do you do it, Luisa? Must be the freckles. Myself, I'd die for a respectable tan and crinkles round the eyes like from creasing them up against the sun and wind, driving the steers west.

'Do you have a boyfriend yet? Who's your boyfriend?' There was a stage when that was all I got from Tina and her gang. They seemed to figure I was going out with Stavros just because we ran the maths club together. Fact was the only thing I ever thought about boys was why didn't they clean them up off the neighborhood along with the garbage. If you really want to know, the only thing I thought about in that way was horses; and then sometimes, girls on horses. Girls in white shirts.

I learned my riding from books. I knew all about holding with my thighs, keeping my knees in and my heels down. I knew about keeping a horse's mouth soft. I knew about blowing in the nostrils too but I didn't bother with that shit. I knew if a horse didn't respond when I hugged it round the neck it wouldn't be worth bothering with nothing else.

114

I knew how it would feel: the clumsiness of all that wide flesh and muscle lumbering under me, the pain in the thighs from controlling it, the tension in my arms from holding the reins firm but light, not holding on for dear life, not pulling, keeping my back straight, keeping my shoulders soft and low. And then, the time when it would happen, when the horse and me would be one, just scoring a channel through the air. I saw myself galloping across plains on a chestnut horse, and sometimes, I have to say, I saw a woman in a white shirt, hair all mussed up, galloping toward me.

Truth of it is, I never had a boyfriend. Never had a girlfriend neither for a long time. Till Pa got laid off and I had to quit high school and find work quick. I started despatch riding. Boring work but I had a whole raft of girlfriends. Must have been the uniform.

Trouble was, they never seemed to be the kind I wanted to stick with. Unconscious, I guess. In all those years I'd only really been stuck on two women. One had run off with her doorman and the other I'd walked out on when I got tired of her taste in music. When you're hot for someone, her passion for country doesn't need to register, but when it cools down a bit and a night at her apartment is less of the rug in front of the fire and more of her friends on the phone and Tammy Wynette, it's time to shake hands on it, I say.

By the time I started with Mary I was twenty-seven and running my own delivery business. Took on some of the boys from my class but I was in command now. Servicing my 'attitude'! It felt real good. Harry was out of a job. That pleased me mightily. Boy, if I was riding past that asshole one dark night!

I'd seen her a few times in bars. She knew some of the women I knew. I doubt I'd ever said more than twenty words to her in five years. When I ran into her at the agency it was something else. I hit the building after hours following a tailback all the way from New Jersey. Someone from a lower floor let me in after I'd been hollering and banging the door for fifteen minutes; I didn't want to have to pass

115

the job on to one of the boys the next day. No one on the Holt and Glaubman reception so I called and she came wandering out of an office in the back and I said hi and she said nothing, just snatched the parcel, so I gave her the sheet to sign. While she was doing it, I took off my helmet and when she gave it me back I said, 'Thanks Mary' and she burst out laughing. It often has an effect on people when I take off the helmet and they see the baby face and the albino hair which starts to curl if I haven't managed to get it cut.

'Jesus Christ,' she said, 'Luisa! Listen, are you through for the day?' She clumped me on my padded shoulder.

'Sure,' I said. 'You better believe it!' I took the sheet from her. 'Mary O'Hara' she'd signed it, big round writing you could read.

'Me too. And I could use a drink.'

She was still laughing as I opened the door for her. She nearly forgot to lock up the offices.

We drank a lot and quickly that evening. I took her to a bar I knew where she wasn't likely to meet any work-mates. It was a Friday night. We were both exhausted and we both had to work the next day. We talked a lot and loud over the music. We just went for it, the way you do some-times when half of it's the beer talking and half of it's the thought that this is a stranger you won't be answering for what you say to for the next month like you would a friend. But maybe some of it was that there came a time, before I got past it, when I wanted to keep on talking for ever, pref-erably with her head beside mine on the pillow.

We went through have you heard about Joanie and Dee, the anti-pornography convention, who did you know in the loft party. We both had friends who'd died in the fire. Soon we were doing the sifted life stories with all the best bits embellished in the way you save up for situations like this. Raunchy anecdotes competing for whose parents were the least understanding, who had the worst teachers, who'd had the most vengeful and vindictive lover. Stories about rows and great dyke fights, who did what to who and who ended up on whose side. We both remembered, breaking out laughing together, why we hadn't been friends before. It was the Margo and Midge rift.

They'd made history, those two. First out dykes to have a number one hit record. Everyone loved them, straight and gay. The trouble had started over Margo's mum. Mrs McKay had been their manager. It was good publicity and all the girls loved it. Margo loved it too until she started telling them the gigs they couldn't do. She wanted them on all the big shows. She wanted them playing Carnegie Hall. But Margo and Midge just wanted to boogie. And they knew if they lost the grassroots, they'd lose everything. Midge cut out. Rock and roll makes a woman impatient. Margo never forgave her. Said it was a race issue. Margo said Midge couldn't handle being managed by a middle-aged black woman whose only training was twenty years running the Rochester All-Saints gospel choir. She said it a lot in interviews. Midge played the clubs and made a couple of albums. She was popular but she never had another hit record. Margo camped up and played the big nite spots and somehow she never lost her cred neither. She wrote good songs. Margo McKay was a success story and we all loved her for it. That and going home every night to her mum, as the publicity had it, and her girlfriend, as only we knew.

What we'd lost was something we'd never seen before. Two beautiful women singing powerful songs together. Two women on stage catching each other's eyes from time to time and holding the gaze in a way that couldn't be mistaken. I'd sided with Midge in that split. Mary had supported Margo. She thought blood was thicker than water. I could feel myself staring at her. She had black hair and green eyes, really green, not just the brown kind that go green with a green sweater. 'I keep persuading myself I haven't sold my soul,' she said. 'I'm just using my talent, But sometimes I get to feeling slimy inside. Something you can't wash out, like tar on your lungs.' I can't remember much past that point. I left my bike and we took a yellow cab back to her apartment because it was nearby and I crashed out on her sofa. The next morning she made us both breakfast and I just watched her in her blue bathrobe with her so green eyes in her pale face and we didn't really know what to say to each other. I left her my card in case she needed a delivery sometime and took the subway back to pick up my bike.

Wasn't long before she called me. Wasn't long before we got close. Wasn't long, to tell the truth, before I was having every kind of damn fantasy about her. I was head over heels. The worst kind of fantasy, the one that goes: 'we are each other's answers'. I guess it was because we shared a major need - to move out of New York. She had kids too. That seemed to fit all right. Two ready-made kids for me to parent. Two kids for me to teach to ride. Me who'd never ridden in my life. I'm not the happy-ever-after type. But I had this hankering after space. When Mary said she couldn't live another year in Manhattan, I got to think I was on the right track.

She bulldozed into my life and I bulldozed into hers. I'd wake up slap bang happy in the mornings at six o'clock, with my chest snapping open and she'd be there inside me, somewhere under my ribs, and I'd feel happy, loud happy, happy like an ox. She was a big woman, big as me, not bony, she was fleshed out, but you could see the bones under her skin. One day, it must have been just after midday and we were still loafing about in bed, just thinking of sending out for a pizza, I'd been regaling her with stories; she'd been regaling me, I felt so in tune with her. Suddenly I looked into her eyes and started to sing, '"Oh, it's the galloping hoofs! It's the green grass rolling range of Wyoming." Holy shit! Mary O'Hara! Jesus, Mary O'Hara. *My Friend Flicka*, *Thunderhead*, *Green Grass of Wyoming*. Did you ever read that stuff? Mary with your glass green eyes? That's what you mean to me. It's a sign,' I said, 'doncha see?' I was thumping the mattress with my fist. 'Mary! Mary, come on, let's do it? It's your big chance too. We can do it together. Honest!'

Mary looked at me, grinning. 'No, I never read those books.'

'You never read them to Sophie and Dan neither?'

'Nope, my kids is inner city retards!'

Matter of fact, Sophie and I had already got off on the wrong foot. She was nine years and sassy and she did not like me staying over. I thought she was a brat. She thought I was a dweeb. When I'd been alone in the house with her one morning she'd come into the bathroom where I was taking a bath and grasped the loose fawcet in both hands.

'I can pull it off.'

'No you can't.'

'You saying I can't do it.'

'I'm saying I don't want you to do it, honey.'

'You don't count, you're not family. You're a dweeb. You got big boobies doncha?'

'Sophie, will you go play with your turtles.'

'You don't like your body, huh? You gotta like your body, Momma says.'

'I like my body fine.'

'I don't.'

'Sophie! You got a sweet little body.'

'No. I mean I don't like yours.'

I guessed this was a relationship I was going to have to work on. Me and Dan Jr though, we got on just fine. He was a cute kid but quiet, a bit serious. Seemed to know what you were thinking sometimes. I'd try and keep my thoughts pure around him. He was going to be my kid I thought. I wanted to put a smile on his face, give him some fun.

I called for Mary at her office one evening, first time I'd been back there since we started. All over the walls were blow-ups of stills from TV ads she'd done. You know the one about the baseball team in their underpants (Persil), the one about the girl on the tightrope (Natracalm) and the one where the Volvo comes right up on you till it's just high focus tyre treads rolling over the screen. That was for Pirelli. Mary made them. She loved her work. She sat talking to a client on the phone. Behind her was a window, backing onto a well. As I watched, large black rag things fell through the air. I had a notion someone was out there on the roof, picking off crows.

'Let's get out of here,' I signed and she sweet-talked her way off the phone.

That evening I could just hear her trying to shout something above the horns and the street noise. 'Okay, Luisa.' It came through my helmet thin as a ring-pull. I turned around and back again fast as her grin cracked into a grimace, and swerved us back in lane. I couldn't wait till we got back to my apartment. I pulled up at Sweeney's and ordered champagne.

'If I heard you wrong, Mary, you're paying for this.'

She grinned and shook her head. 'Believe it!' she said softly and we linked arms and drank through them. When she'd downed a glass, she put her elbows on the table and rested her head on them. 'Okay, honey, we'll go. I'm slowing up anyway, have to make notes of things I used to hold in my head. Let's go before they fire me, huh?'

We finished the bottle, grabbed a take-out, went back to my apartment, showered together and went to bed for a hug-up. We had a couple of beers with the food and watched TV sitting with our arms round each other.

Now I loved Mary. Have I said that? And I knew the gods don't mess around giving two opportunities to a woman who doesn't take one. Wyoming it was going to be. We got an agent to scout for places and he sent us a whole lot of glitzy purpose-built things till we began to feel crazy and then relieved that it wasn't going to happen but about fifty-nine abusive phone calls later we got the specifications on a place with photos that made us call up and say, 'Hold it, when can we see it?'

The Robin Ranch it was called. And it was perfect. Out of a book: all on one storey, but the ground level changed, following the contours of the earth below; it was soft pink granite and the door was bright blue and it opened straight into the living room. No cows in sight. My kind of a ranch. We put up the deposit on it right there and then.

I sold the business almost overnight and realized it could have fetched a lot more. I'd been sitting on a goldmine.

It made me feel kind of secure, knowing I'd built that up in three years. Mary put her brownstone on the market and set about negotiating a consultancy with Holt and Glaubman while she worked out her notice. We would get her the technology: PC and fax, so she could work from home. It was when I was round at her house one evening poring over computer magazines after the kids had gone to bed that she told me she was planning on leaving them with their father.

'Mary! We're going to Wyoming! You're going to leave those kids in New York? I don't believe this!'

'They'll be okay. They're in private school. If they don't want to stay with Danny, they can board.'

'Shit! How come I never knew this? Do you have a wealthy family or something?'

'Danny's in gilts.'

'Jesus!'

'Luisa. Will you listen to me? We are doing *your* dream. I'm coming with you because I love you. I'm not taking my kids away from school. They can come visit.'

So that was the arrangement. I soon learned there was no point arguing with Mary and it was a relief in one way. I got on fine with little Dan but Sophie was something else. Mary and I moved out to our ranch and took a week's vacation decorating it. We turned the room next to the living room into her study and by the beginning of the following week she was working there. Before the month was up I'd taken off west to buy my horse. Finished up with two. A chestnut mare, sixteen hands, star on her forehead, one white stocking, and her black foal. I drove over every day and she taught me how to ride the mare and train up the colt. She said I was a natural.

I called the mare Schooner because she sailed; she took the wind into her. I called the colt Sam. Every morning I'd wake early, the light was so penetrating, make us both some toast and coffee and bring it back to bed. I'd put my arms round Mary and kiss her neck or shoulder till she woke, turning to me with little humming noises. Sometimes the breakfast would get cold, but often we'd just eat and get straight up to work. I'd go out to the ponies and give them their feed and ride out on Schooner.

There was something about being alone out there, riding all morning. Surrounded by silence, silence broken by clean sound, animal cries and scuffles, the wind, the big birds screeching. I'd ride over hillside, through forest, from one clearing to another. She'd pick out the way with her delicate feet, lifting her knees like a Spanish-trained horse and I'd talk to her. She'd prick her ears and raise her head and shake the tackle around. Sometimes we'd stop on a peak and just take in the country. I'd let her choose when we stopped. My Indian Paint. I'd get off and hug her round the neck and put my face up to her face to take in the hot breath of her and get a feel of that soft muzzle. And if I'd squint hard into the wide distant horizon with the wind watering my eyes up, the colours would stain into each other and drop onto my lunch. Sometimes I'd still be crying when we rode off again. All that peace and fullness just seeping out of the landscape and smacking me in the mouth. I cried so much she must have wondered what was happening but Schooner just put her two ears up straight and a little wide so I'd know she was on alert but she never so much as flicked them or turned her head unless I was gulping words.

The feel of that horse beneath me was everything I'd always dreamed. It was like I'd done it in another life. The way I learned to ride so quick too. That's what made me sad. Thinking about the life I'd really lived and what everybody had to cope with back home. Have to be so smart no one dare comment on your tacky year-before-last outfit, or ask do you got video. I did it in 'attitude', Tina used laughs. I missed her. Even missed her dumb gang. Mikey had 'heart'. That's what the kids called it these days; it meant you weren't afraid of no one and you had to show it.

I knew I'd not relaxed in the whole of my life till then; been on alert against letting the shame show. Alone in the wide space now, the memories went ticking loud through my head till sometimes it seemed they'd bust it. Like they were clamoring to get out and fill the big air. So I let the tears come out where the wind could take them. It was something about me and Mary too and the way we were getting so close. Our lovemaking turned me inside out, babied me, I was softening up. I was so happy I could have died every day. I'd get back and feed and groom the horses, take a shower, fix us both something to eat and then I'd set to work on the house: scraping, filling, plastering, drilling, sawing, painting and papering. There was one of those sixties covers they kept playing on the radio that summer, something about love lifting us up where we belong and that's what I'd be singing.

Mary was working hard. She was working her bones out but she had to establish herself. She was doing fine and I admired her for it. Nothing I love better in the whole world than seeing a woman go for it and get there. She'd be at her desk by six o'clock most days; she'd done a day's work by midday, nearly two by six o'clock in the evening when we hit a few beers and watched TV. Me, I was just doing what the gods had in mind for me, and taking my time about it. I knew I could make myself another business okay and the more it had to do with my horses, the better I'd like it.

Then came the morning when Mary heard she'd got the new Audi account; just about the most prestigious thing the agency had to offer. The most sophisticated new machine to hit the road in ten years, light, and low like a sports car but strong as a Volvo truck. This time she'd need to make a journey - go back to New York to see the car being trialled and co-ordinate the rest of the creative team. She started walking round flexing her fingers in and out of fists and whistling through her top teeth. I guessed she was happy.

She booked a flight for the following day; it was important to show them you could move quick as anyone, no point hanging around. She was going to take a week off, stay with a friend in the Village, see the kids, drop in on Danny. She spent three hours solid on the phone.

'How's he making out?' I asked when we finally sat down to a little farewell dinner I'd been working on. 'With the kids and all, I mean.'

'Danny's fine. He works on Wall Street for god's sake.'

'And I been meaning to ask you, Mary, how in the name of Jesus you got hitched with a guy like that?'

'He was the brightest boy in college. He used to make me laugh.'

'Sunshine marriage, huh!'

'No, Luisa, it was misery. Sheer hell and humiliation. He used to manacle me to the bedpost. He used to make me wash the diapers by hand.'

'You're kidding!'

'Listen Luisa, it was a regular marriage. We had some good times. We raised two beautiful children. It just didn't last, that's all.'

'Because you were living a lie.'

'Tell you the truth, I was living just the way I'd always wanted. Wish I'd never got Deirdre Malley's fingers down my pants.'

I was grinning at her but she didn't want any. 'Bernie's seven months pregnant,' she continued. 'Guess they thought it was bad karma to tell me before. Might put my wicked fairy spell on them. No choice now. I'd see soon enough or the kids'd tell me.'

'Oh Mary, what about we look after them while she goes into hospital? They'd love it here!'

'You wanna look after them?'

'Sure.'

'I'll ask, sweetheart, that's a promise.'

'I'll keep my fingers crossed.'

Soon as she was gone I started to fret. Spent most of my time grooming Schooner and her fattening foal, talking to them, playing with them, starting to put Sam through his paces. I started scheming too - how I was going to set up a a riding stables, no, a breeding stud, no some kind of fancy wild west heritage rodeo thing. She never rang for three days. When she did I couldn't stop her talking.

'You're not going to believe this, Luisa, my budget

is megabucks. This one's opera. I'm going raw, this time. Shameless. You'll hate it. Panther, right? You never saw nothing so sleek. You can see all the muscles, tendons, veins, all that stuff, moves like greased lightning in fur, okay. Here's how we start. Drum roll, huge crack sound and we're between mountains. Dark, dark blue. Then close up to the animal's eyes, bright green in the dark and gradually we can make out the outline, yeah? Of its face. Then it jumps over the camera and another camera takes it running from in front and the light comes up. Cut to the guy driving hell for leather through the dawn; he's in the same landscape but it dissolves into a town and he drives to this like frontiersville really smart commodities bank and it's so early he's wiping the dew off his face, you know, and the doors move apart for him and there's a woman standing there, short black dress, long black gloves, and she says, "I knew you'd make it," and he puts a hand on her shoulder and motions with his head and she takes him through to the conference room which is all set out ready and he takes the chair and she...'

'Sounds like Danny's kind of car, Mary!'

'Didn't think you'd like it.'

'It's gross!'

''S gonna make us wealthy though, put me on the road! Ha!'

'When you coming back? I miss you.'

'Listen, I'm not getting on too hot with Bernie, neither's Dan Jr. In fact, he's not getting on with anyone. He said if I didn't take him back to the ranch, he was going to run away. Fact is I need to stay on a bit here, Luisa. He said he didn't mind hanging out with you for a bit and you could teach him to be a cowboy.'

'Great!'

'Don't teach him to use a gun huh!'

'You tell Dan Jr. I'd be honoured. Might even throw

in a spot of lasso-ing. How's he gonna get here?'

'Plane. They look after the kids. Pick him up off the steward at the airport. Tomorrow?'

I was laughing. 'Ring me the details. I'll be there.'

I went out and fixed the training rope to Sam. His mouth was soft and his manners docile; I was having some trouble getting him to jump. But he'd suit little Dan. I walked him round the paddock, trotted him, took him over the low jumps. Then I saddled up Schooner and took him along with us. I hadn't done this as often as I ought to. It meant reining Schooner into a trot when I wanted to give her her head but she always knew what was expected of her, and Sam was coming on nice enough. Dan Jr could feed him and groom him and get to know him. Then one day we'd put him on his back.

I collected Dan from our one horse airport. He looked kinda taller than I remembered and his eyes had gotten smaller in his face - light brown eyes that glinted green in the sun. I wanted to lift him in the air and swing him round but I took a grip on myself.

'Morning Daniel.'

'Hi Aunt Luisa.'

'Hi, son.' Neither him nor his big sister never called me 'aunt' before. I took his case and walked him to the car. He fell quiet as we drove beween the timbered mountain ranges and I wondered was he frightened. Later, as we hit the road between the planes, fading now to taupe and fawn as the summer grew on apace, I guessed the scenery was speaking to his soul. In the distance we could see the sharp red granite drops, the mesas, and the black silhouettes of birds wheeling and dropping through the sky.

That boy took to the ranch like it was summmer camp. He fell in with working around the place and started to get some color come up in his face. He was careful, kind and considerate. I figured they could teach manners at this private school; he wasn't like no boy I ever grew up with.

Best of all, he took to Sam like I hadn't dared hope. He was up in the mornings at six o'clock, feeding him and brushing his mane and tail out. By the way he rouged up when I drew near I reckoned he'd been talking to the colt, and I figured he was saying things he couldn't tell no one else.

Sam wasn't used to no rider but Dan couldn't wait, said he'd asked the pony if he could get on his back and Sam had given him a sign. So I fixed a saddle on the colt and Dan J climbed up and sure enough, Sam stood there like he'd been waiting for it and when I led them round the yard on the training rope, he walked, meek as a lamb, while Dan stroked his neck and rubbed his face in his mane, going, 'There, boy, that's my pony.'

But over supper he started to get rude and I realized what an effort he'd made. 'Why can't Mom look after us?' he said,

'Why's she have to come out here?'

'Oh Dan!' I went to put my arms round him but he ran off to his room. I could hear his sobs from the kitchen. I waited five minutes then warmed some milk and took it across to his room but he wouldn't take it.

'Hey, Dan J,' I said. 'Your mom *loves* you and Sophie. She really misses you, she couldn't wait to get back to New York to see you all again.'

'She never asked if we wanted to come with her to the ranch house.'

'She didn't want to break up your schooling.'

'I don't wanna be at school, I want to be here.'

'Hey, Dan, I love you being here, but it's an hour's drive to the nearest school and it's nothing like the school you're at now.'

'I don't care. I *belong* here.'

'You're a fine boy, Dan J, it's a pleasure to have you here.'

He relaxed in my arms.

He started to talk more after that evening and when he went quiet I didn't pry. I'd promised him I wouldn't tell on nothing he'd said and I wouldn't. He was riding real pretty on his own now, sitting straight and using the reins nice and tender with Sam's young mouth. I could envision us one day, galloping side by side across the prairies and I figured it wouldn't be long, the way he was picking up. First, I'd have to get Sam used to the open country. Meanwhile, I took the boy out sometimes on Schooner, letting him hold on round my waist while I reined her into a canter. I was careful as hell because I had forebodings in that country, fear that the birds hanging so high in the air held us in some kind of design, and I'd say, 'Hold on tight, son.' But I knew that if he didn't ride that country a few times, the red clay soil, the little ditches and watercuts, the sudden jutting hills, the steep red drops, the solitary wind-battered pines, he wouldn't get the ache to be back in it.

Dan stayed ten days. I thought he'd grow bored, pining for his friends but he just lay on the floor watching TV when he was tired. I never made him switch channels and I never had another tear out of him. Night-times I read him *My Friend Flicka*. He'd asked Mary on one of her phone calls if I could go back with him and we'd agreed between us to share the money for the flight. I wanted to make sure not one thing happened to that boy before he was back in his mom's sight. And nothing did. He fell asleep on the plane and I put an arm round him and he lay on my lap peaceful as a cat.

It happened to me. I went home, hoped I'd see Tina. She wasn't there. Just Mom and Mikey. Mikey glared at me and simpered, then slunk off.

'Siddown,' said Mom, watching him out. 'Ya come just the right time, girl, Mikey's in trouble, off school. Ya father beat the boy and his heart won't stand it.'

'What'd he do?'

'Beat up on another boy on account of he dirtied his sneakers.'

128

'Bad?'

'Kid got two broken ribs, perforated eardrum, broken nose.' She sniffed. 'Leastways that boy got heart. Valor. Don't need to run away from the neighborhood in shame. Live like man and wife with your ladyfriend'.

'Calm down, Momma.'

'I knew from the minute you was born. What I done wrong my lord, get an infant look like this? All the color washed out of her. Never got no better. Never can bring myself to kiss you girl, wondering did ya wash your face good since ...?'

I grabbed hold of her shoulders and shouted into her face: 'You keep it under wraps when I'm around.'

'Mikey!' she yelled.

Mikey was in the kitchen in seconds. I loosed my grip on her.

'Well, it's the wild west hero.' He walked by me and ran a thumb down my neck. 'Nice tits though.'

I swung out, he ducked, I grazed his ear.

'Jus' bein' friendly, big sis.' He relaxed against the wall and as he turned his head to finger the ear I saw how his head went into one big fold where his hair was shaved off at the back.

'I wanna put him through college,' said Mom. 'I figured you might help out, Luisa.'

I couldn't speak for a minute. I gathered myself together, looked at my watch. 'I got a plane to catch,' I said, 'I don't have no money to spare.'

I tell you one thing life taught me. If you're poor you need culture. I'm not talking wall to wall books, I'm not talking theatre and dinner at fancy restaurants. I'm talking something you make up yourself or with your friends, something that tells you who you are and gives you respect. Don't just go for what you ain't got; that's the grief ticket.

I wrote this on the plane. I wrote it to Mikey. I thought, Okay, but I'll never see you or Mom or Pa ever again - none of you, excepting Tina. I'll pay your way, though no one never paid mine and I'd sooner tear your balls off. I stepped back in the nightmare and I stepped right out again. I done my crying. There's people get destroyed by their families. Not me. I'm the riding off into the sunset type.

KISS THE BOYS GOODBYE

HELEN SANDLER

She stood in the centre of the ring of cards. Spread around her feet were the magical images of queens, kings, the Hermit, the Sun, a Page on horseback. A magnificent naked woman stood in the sea holding aloft a giant golden goblet.

Marilyn felt the energy of the circle, of the force that had guided these particular cards from the pack of seventy-eight. It was two o'clock in the morning. Her optimism and excitement were taking over where her limbs and intellect were tiring. The message in the tarot cards was clear, she must use her current upsurge of joy and hopefulness to creative ends, she must cast aside destructive influences.

'If it were the middle of the day,' she thought, 'I'd call Coral and tell her I don't want to carry on this craziness any longer. I might even tell her it's over. Then I'd start that painting.'

But instead it was the middle of the night. And it was best to make a record of the tarot before acting on it.

She fetched her Polaroid Instant from the bedroom and took several pictures of the tarot cards, the lovely round depiction of her total state of mind and body, of her place in the scheme of things. The photos appeared from the slit like babies. She tidied the cards into their box and sat on the floor watching the photos dry into blueprints for a painting.

Yes, there was no need now to launch into the painting of conflict and masked creatures that bubbled in her brain. Instead she would try to capture what she had seen and felt in the cards. No point in going up to the large cold room that she used as a studio. She would work there tomorrow

131

in the flood of daylight from the bay window.

Right now she picked up a sketchpad from the coffee table without getting up from the living room floor. She was feeling comfortable with her body, and happy in this room of pine and paintings, scattered with the gifts and trinkets of thirty-six years of survival.

She smiled, rolling a pencil towards her across the table. 'I must stop calling it survival,' she said out loud, 'I'm living, I'm enjoying myself, not just breathing.'

She let the smile stay on her face, and picked out the Ace of Cups swiftly on the paper, with a few soft lines: sea, sky, woman, cup. She would dawdle over it tomorrow, experiment with blues, perhaps decorate the goblet. Then she would move on to a more abstract vision of the card. This card represented her current upsurge of emotion and feelings, and was the first card in the spread, in the First House, the position of Self, the outward personality.

This card sometimes signified a new relationship, or the revival of an old one. Marilyn wondered if some old flame would replace Coral, then reproached herself for her flippancy. The girl was just starting out, she could not be cast aside so easily. It would take time and kindness to end this relationship, and for the first time since she had realized the affair was drawing to a close, Marilyn felt that she did have a reserve of patience hiding in her heart that could be given to Coral.

But what a fool she had been to get involved - for the sake of excitement and sex and the breaking of taboos - with a girl of eighteen. She was still shocked by the very thought of Coral's age. She was still incapable of referring to her as a woman, except when Coral's presence demanded it.

She moved on to the card that challenged her to deal directly with Coral - the image of The Lovers....

The pencil scraped across the page and she let out a sharp cry of shock. The telephone's ring had invaded this safe place. Marilyn let her breathing start to settle back to normal and felt the tingle of fear linger in her nerve endings. The electronic noise continued and she grabbed at the phone.

'Marilyn?'

'What are you doing ringing now? Christ, Coral, I nearly jumped through the ceiling.'

'You were awake then?'

'Awake, and sitting quietly. But now that you've called we may as well talk.'

'What do you mean?' The younger woman was nervous now. 'You don't even know why I phoned. What do you mean by "talk"? You always sound so ominous when you say things like that.'

'What do you expect me to sound like at three o'clock in the morning? You have no respect for my time, my sleep, my need for quiet.'

'I rang for a *reason*!'

Marilyn heard angry tears in Coral's voice and cursed herself for jumping straight into this pattern of attack and defence and abandoning the promises she had just made to herself to be kinder to her lover. Now the girl would weep endlessly and Marilyn would hate her, and hate herself, and not sleep all night....

'All right,' she said, 'tell me why you rang.'

'I couldn't sleep, I...'

'Coral, I hope this isn't just some cure for insomnia.'

'Listen,' her voice was a whine, 'listen, Marilyn, please - I'm, I'm pregnant.'

Pause. Consider. Think. I am not the father of her child. Somebody must be. Will I have to give her a large sum of money? Is that it? Or adopt the child? Oh God, this is completely ludicrous...

'Coral this is completely ludicrous. You don't just suddenly realize at 3 am that you haven't had a period lately. What's going on?'

Anger, fear and confusion came back down the

phone. 'I'm going to have a baby! Never mind what fucking time of the night it is! I just got up and did the test. I didn't want to do it when anyone was around, in case I told them all about it, so I waited...' Coral was sobbing uncontrollably.

'You,' Marilyn started to shout without raising her voice, something she had learned in teacher training college a long time ago, 'You have slept with a man, Coral, you have slept with someone other than me and you can take the bloody consequences because it has *nothing* to do with me. Don't phone me again.'

Around nine, Marilyn woke with the smell of whisky hanging over her. She realized it was coming from her mouth. The beauty and calm and hope of the tarot reading had been desecrated by her crazy girl lover, and she had scotched out the guilt and switched out the light after ripping the phone wire from the socket.

Now, in those first moments of memory and grasping desperately at the day ahead, she saw that she knew nothing of Coral's story.

She called the hall of residence, not giving herself time to reconsider, and asked for the room number that Coral was sharing with a foetus. There was an interval of a full five minutes before Coral - whose room was two doors from the payphone - murmured hello into the receiver.

'I'm sorry. I'm sorry Coral, it was late. Do you want to tell me properly what's happening?'

'I've told you.'

'Who, how... I mean, how did you get pregnant?'

'Well I didn't go down the sperm bank with a milk bottle.'

It was slightly reassuring to hear some life in her voice.

'Look, love, when you're ready, come round here and we'll have a proper talk.'

'What day is it?'

'It's Sunday.'

'So how will I get across London? I'm not standing for twenty-four hours on the platform at fucking Finchley Road and Frognal.'

'Get a cab, Coral. I'll pay.'

'I don't know.' There was a firmness in the younger woman's voice that was rare. 'I'm not sure I want to see you.'

Marilyn swallowed the words that were ready in her mouth - 'Don't do me any favours'. Instead she said, 'See how you feel when you're properly awake. Take care.'

She put the phone down and went down to the front room to look at her work of the night before. She was a little disappointed to see just one completed drawing - the Woman in the Water. She picked up the polaroids and an echo of the positive energy of the tarot reading buzzed through her.

She decided to do some more work on the idea. Even in her present mood she could do some preparation, and when the 'upsurge of emotion' returned, as it surely would, she would be ready to start painting.

As she brushed her teeth and made some coffee, she couldn't keep her mind off Coral. Would she come round later? If so, Marilyn would try to talk calmly with her, get more information and even try to give some advice. She seldom made links between Coral's life and how her own had been at that age - it usually only served to emphasize how young her lover was. But now Marilyn reminded herself of her own unwanted pregnancy in her early twenties, and the horror and relief of her miscarriage.

She gathered up the pack of tarot cards, the photographs and sketches, and headed upstairs. Half of her still just wanted to be rid of Coral - who became more of a liability by the day - and what better opportunity than this?

A jealous ache nagged at her. The girl didn't just fuck some man, she had to ring Marilyn and tell her so.

She turned on the radio to drown these thoughts.

135

Why get in this state when she had already planned to end the relationship?

She adjusted the drawing board.

Coral arrived soon after lunch, with no sign of a taxi. She looked lachrymose and vulnerable. Though taller than Marilyn, everything about her today suggested a small scared person, perhaps a child, dressed in sweatshirt and jeans. Marilyn wanted to ruffle her hair, tell her not to worry. She stopped herself.

Coral was moving her arms about too much, as if she had expected a hug.

'Come in, do you want a drink?'

'Yeah, coffee please.' She took a rollup from behind her ear and lit it as she went into the kitchen. Then she made herself as small as possible in the wicker chair.

They were silent as Marilyn made the drinks. The kitchen was small, and it was almost painful to stay quiet, with nowhere to look except at each other or a wall. Marilyn sat down at the table as if in a library. Coral scrunched out her cigarette, unwound herself for long enough to pick up her bag from the floor, and began to roll another of the thin tubes. With great restraint, Marilyn made no comment on either the chainsmoking or the tiny amount of tobacco involved. She wanted to say 'Treat yourself to another strand.'

But then, she wanted to say a great many things, most of them contradictory. To express kindness and malice, concern and disinterest, jealousy and an eager non-monogamy. It even occurred to her to tell Coral not to touch another cigarette for the sake of the foetus.

Eventually she heard herself speak. 'So, do you want to talk about it?'

'Uh-huh. I guess so. It's just, you're...'

'What?'

'You're not making it very easy.' Coral looked at Marilyn as if she expected her to hit her.

She looked pathetic, and Marilyn was stoked suddenly with loathing for such weakness. For the dependency and fear that she saw in Coral's eyes, which made it so easy to manipulate her, to get what she wanted while losing all respect for her lover.

Marilyn's neck muscles tightened as she tried to make a calm reply. 'This is difficult for me too, Coral. Tell me who he is, what's going on.'

'Do you want to know?'

'No. Not really. I don't want to think about you making love with some young man and then coming round here, perhaps the next night, and licking my cunt.'

'Stop it! It's not like that. God, Marilyn, I should never have come.' The girl's eyes filled with dribbling tears.

Perhaps this was a mistake. Marilyn was engulfed by it all, sinking fast into the suffocating pattern of their practised exchanges, where she always maintained control and hated herself for it. Like a chess grandmaster pitched against the same young beginner again and again, she longed for Coral to play some unexpected move. Even when it was Coral who called check and she herself screamed out in defeat or confusion, the girl's fear of what she had done left Marilyn in control.

'Here,' she said with effort, pushing a box of tissues towards Coral. 'You're here now, let's try and talk. Tell me from the beginning, whatever there is to tell. Not as a lover, as a - ' she could barely say the word, 'as a friend.'

Coral looked at her, as if she would rather place her trust in the Prime Minister. She lit the new cigarette and the smell of sweet damp tobacco calmed them both.

'It's difficult to explain what happened,' she began, loosening a leg from the knot of her body, 'and, like, well, I don't want to upset you...' She blew her nose. 'But like you say, I'm here now.' She smiled weakly at Marilyn, who put her hand out on impulse and stroked Coral's shoulder.

'Well, I've told you before I don't want to sleep with anyone but you. It was true. I mean, it is true. But... well, about six weeks ago there was this party in college and I went along on my own. And there was this bloke there. Richard. We were chatting, joking around. Then I started to feel a bit sick and I said I was going to bed. He said he'd come back and make me some coffee. I wasn't sure. I mean, I hardly knew him, but I wasn't in a fit state to argue and he seemed perfectly nice.

'So we went to my room. And as soon as we got in the door he started to kiss my face - it just seemed funny. God, Marilyn, I can't even remember properly - I can't even believe what happened. The room was going round, and his face was just grinning on and on and I couldn't think what to do except that I might be sick. He took my clothes off and I so wanted to believe he was putting me to bed...' She started to cry and so did Marilyn.

Marilyn stumbled to her feet and wrapped her arms round Coral.

'I never said no,' she sobbed into Marilyn's belly, 'I never said anything at all.'

'Don't talk any more, love,' Marilyn swallowed her tears and held Coral tight. 'We can talk more later if you want to. You just cry all you need to. Do you want to lie down?'

'Yes.'

Marilyn scooped her up from the chair and carried her in her arms, a small thin bundle, up the stairs. She tucked Coral under the duvet.

'Sing to me. Sing that 'I was thirty-seven'.' Coral wiped at her face and smiled, 'That always cheers me up.'

She looked as if she needed to cry for a fortnight rather than cheer up on the spot, but Marilyn began the old pop song that made them laugh, written as it was for a man to sing about a girl:

> 'I was thirty-seven, you were seventeen,
> You were half my age, a youth I'd never seen,
> Unlikely people meeting in a dream,
> Heaven only knows the way it should have been...'

And she launched into the chorus before she realized that it was even more ironic than usual:

> *Come live with me*
> *- Kiss the boys goodbye...*

'Oh God, Coral, it's not that funny after all.'

But her lover was still smiling as a couple more tears formed in her eyes. 'Never mind, I like it when you sing.'

Marilyn leant over her and stroked her hair, humming softly until she fell asleep.

The pencil shavings were dropping into the big red bin in the studio when Coral called from the next room.

'Marilyn?'

'Yes, love?' She put down the crayons and went into the bedroom, where Coral's face above the covers was pink and swollen from crying.

'Can we do the tarot? I need to think properly about this baby.'

'It's not a baby yet.'

'Give it time.'

'I'm surprised you haven't given it more time,' said Marilyn, with more vehemence than she had intended. Then, 'You should have told me about it when it happened.'

'I couldn't. I couldn't tell anyone, least of all you. I thought you'd react - well, like you did last night. How did it go? "You have slept with someone other than me and you can take the bloody consequences..." '

'I'm sorry,' Marilyn interrupted, 'really Coral I am so sorry. But I didn't know...'

'But that's it you see, I didn't think it would make any difference if I explained it all or not. I should never have let it happen, I'd been unfaithful to you, I felt guilty and angry and unhappy - '

139

'I'm not surprised!' Marilyn exclaimed sympathetically.

'No, it would be hard to surprise you, you've seen it all before.'

'Well, if you feel like that why did you ever tell me?'

'I was bound to tell you eventually,' Coral was resigned now rather than angry, 'I tell you all sorts of things I should probably keep to myself. I can't help it.'

'I'm honoured I'm sure.' Marilyn's bitter tone was undercut by the familiar smile that flickered on her face, and Coral sighed.

She made herself comfortable in the bed. 'I couldn't tell you earlier,' she explained, 'You were away on the Great Narrowboat Expedition, and when you got back I'd already buried the whole experience. I just pretended it hadn't been... bad. And went home for the Easter holidays. By the time I got back a month later I even wanted to have sex. And you know how irregular my periods are. Then it dawned on me. And it's made me think about it again, remember it. It makes me feel ill, Marilyn.'

Marilyn was thinking of the happy-go-lucky barge holiday with Julie, their sketching and cooking and chat, the sun more plentiful than expected in April. And all the time Coral had been answering her ten pence calls with, 'Yes, I'm fine, enjoy yourself.'

'We should go out,' she said, 'Get some fresh air.'

Coral nodded, and Marilyn knew that they would somehow contrive to do that tarot reading first.

The drive to Hampstead Heath from Forest Hill is not a short one. Yet it was not until they drove across the river, saw the solid buildings lined along the gold-grey flow, crossed the divide between south London dyke and north London dyke...

'Coral, those cards.'

'Uh-huh.'

'They were all 'starting out' cards, and 'making a

choice' cards.'

'Mine usually are. I'm starting out on my adult life, aren't I? A route packed with choices.'

Marilyn flinched at the cynicism in her voice.

'The Page of Cups. The way he looks at his own reflection in the water. Narcissism. But also loving yourself first, learning to live with yourself, before you can fully love others.'

'Marilyn! I saw the card, all right? I asked the tarot about the baby. That's just part of the answer, what you've just said. Even from *that* card, you could say..., 'If I have the kid, it will be partly to have a reflection of myself.'

'But us!' thought Marilyn. 'I'm trying to talk about us. I'm trying to get out of this relationship while I love you, while we're close.'

She took a right too sharply and the little blue car shuddered. Coral patted her benignly.

'Fuck it! Fuck it, Coral, you wouldn't know a thing about the tarot if I hadn't shown you.'

'You taught me everything I know. Remind me to thank you some time.'

Ask me what's the matter! Marilyn was straining to breathe with the effort of withholding this demand. Ask me, she wanted to say, ask me and I will tell you all.

Coral turned back to her, trying to cheer her up, and asked, 'Is the frisbee still in the boot?'

The frisbee was still in the boot, and they frisbeed it back and forth between them, on the walk to the Women's Pond. There, enclosed by trees and hedges, women lay clothed or bare-breasted on the grass, or swam in the pond beneath the watchful eye of the butch lifeguard.

Coral immediately made her clothes as minimalist as possible, and as she pulled off her trousers and rolled up her top, Marilyn noticed for the first time the swelling of her belly, the slight enlargement of her round breasts. The newness, the change, drew her to Coral. She would have liked to express delight, to marvel, but it was so inappropriate that she just slumped to the ground and feigned irritation.

'What is going on with you, Marilyn? There's not much point in going out for fresh air if you're going to behave like this all afternoon. I'd have been better off with an air freshener.'

'I'll tell you what's going on. I'm in a bad mood. I'm sad, I'm angry. We're not communicating.'

'So communicate.'

'I just feel that we don't talk about things.'

'Well we don't always have to talk about everything. We talked today, anyway.' Coral was sombre.

'But we should have talked earlier.'

'Fucking hell, Marilyn, don't start that again.'

'But think about it, Coral. What sort of relationship are we having if you couldn't even tell me you'd been raped?'

'I hadn't been raped.'

'Okay, so what kind of relationship is it if you can have sex with a man while I'm on holiday?'

'Just because I say I wasn't raped doesn't mean I wanted to have sex with him.'

'Really? Should I tell you the feminist definition of rape?'

'Shut up!' Coral snapped. 'Stop pissing around, Marilyn. This isn't some clever debate at the London Women's Centre. Let *me* decide what happened to *me*. I was there.'

Marilyn glared at the girl and stood up to put on her swimming costume. All around were women with friends or lovers their own age.

She strode to the pond without a backward glance, and slid in to the water, gasping from the cold. She set off at a fast crawl, thoughts going through her head in rhythm with her strokes: 'I still love her. We don't get on. I want her body.'

Marilyn turned onto her back and propelled herself slowly around the middle of the pond, watching the clouds. She had surprised herself. For some time she had been avoiding thoughts of sex with Coral. They made love rarely and passionately, screaming and grasping each other. It was always incredibly intense and they always had a row a couple of hours later. There was no point in longing for it at other times, and so she didn't.

'What is this?' she thought, as she brushed past another swimmer without apology. 'It feels like sexual jealousy. I'm jealous of a rapist. I'm turned on by her pregnancy. When the Women's Liberation Movement sucked me in, no one warned me about this. No one said, "Sister, theory is one thing - feelings are another." The very act of raising my consciousness was supposed to dispel these kinds of thoughts...'

As she swam back to the side, Marilyn wondered briefly if Coral might have gone home. But no, from her vantage point on the concrete she could see a teenage figure curled around a magazine, smoking. She went into the shower block and splashed tokenistically under the spray.

Coming out she saw a woman rise out of the water like her sketch of the Ace of Cups, full of energy.

Walking slowly over to Coral, shivering, she tried to control her breathing. 'I have to finish this today,' she thought, 'I really have to finish with her.'

'All right?' she asked.

'I'm all right,' Coral replied, glancing up for a second. 'You're the one who stormed off.'

'Going to swim?'

'Not until I'm sure I want a miscarriage. It looks like melted ice in there.'

'It's not hot.' She sprawled out next to Coral, feeling the warmth of the sun on her wet body.

They were quiet for perhaps two minutes, pretending calm, until Marilyn turned over and lay dripping above Coral. She kissed her full on the lips and Coral's eyes opened wide in surprise or excitement as she opened her mouth to Marilyn's tongue and pulled her down on top of her.

Oh God, the sudden ache returning from nowhere, her wet costume getting wetter, Marilyn wanted to carry Coral to the nearest bed as she had this morning. She stood up, rubbed a towel over her body and pulled on her shirt. She wrapped the towel around her waist and helped Coral to her feet, as one should a lover, as one should a pregnant woman.

They ran across half the Heath to the car, drove dangerously through the Hampstead side streets, past the homes of the rich and famous to the college. Marilyn parked abruptly on the residential street that separated the two halves of the campus. They walked through an arch, and across a lawn to one wing of the imposing ivy-covered Hall, then up three flights of stairs. Marilyn seldom visited the Hall, full as it was of bright and over-enthusiastic young women and their self-conscious men friends. Even now, in the heat of the day and of her passion, she felt too old to be entering this warm little room, with its standard wooden furniture and posters supporting armed struggle in Central America, Ireland, South Africa.

She turned to her lover - for were they not still lovers? - and saw her own longing for Coral reflected in her face. They had hardly spoken as they hurtled through the streets but now she said, 'God, I want you,' and Coral nodded and wrapped her arms around her, held tight and kissed her so slowly that Marilyn cried out.

The room faded, the fact that girls were giggling in corridors now that the sun had cooled did not stop Marilyn from screaming when Coral plunged careful fingers deep inside her. She screamed with the relief, the release, the close soft loving touch of the woman she had felt so distant from. And when she had finished screaming, she gently licked Coral's tight body, rubbed a warm hand over the rounded belly, licked at her cunt which today tasted sweet and salty. They moved slowly together, with a sharp energy like the definitive words of an unhurried farewell.

And when they lay in the semi-darkness of evening, and ignored a knock at the door, Coral stroked Marilyn's face and said quietly,

'It's over isn't it?'

'I don't know.'

'I know. Let's quit while we're ahead.' And Marilyn felt Coral's soft kiss on her cheek and saw a tear run down her face.

She closed her eyes. 'It's over, isn't it,' she repeated in her head, and hard dry sobs rose from deep in her stomach and coughed through her body. Like choking. Like grief.

Coral kissed her once more, got up, and put a tape on. The melancholy song was somehow soothing. Billie Holliday, it sounded like. Marilyn's tears finally came loose and dropped out, one by one. She smiled.

'I was supposed to tell you it was over.'

Coral sniffed and grinned, standing at the edge of the bed looking down at her. 'Beat you to it.'

By the time Billie had crooned her last tune, Marilyn was pulling her trousers from her bag and stepping into them.

'Listen, love, we'll have to have a proper session about the small question of the - well, that lump.'

'You make it sound like stomach cancer. It's a baby,' said Coral, 'And I know what I'm going to do. How can I possibly bring up a child? No home, no plans, no cash. I'm going to get an abortion. Well, try to.'

'I'm sorry. I mean, I'm sorry you'll have to... go through that.'

Coral hugged her. 'Perhaps if I hurry up and get on

with it, before it's too late, I won't have too much time to worry about it. I'll go to the advisory place tomorrow. Then I'll talk to you - maybe meet for a drink if you're free?'

'Yes, good idea.'

They kept smiling. Marilyn almost started to cry again, but she swallowed it and grinned inanely to fill the silence.

'Come on then,' Coral said, 'I'll walk you to the car.'

The car. When they reached it Marilyn wanted to pull Coral into it and drive off into the night with her. She opened the hatchback and took out the sketch of the Woman in the Water from among the drawings she had thought she might work on at the Heath.

'It's the Ace of Cups,' she said, holding it up to the light inside the car. 'I want you to have it. She stands for...'

'...An upsurge of emotions and feelings, a foundation to build upon,' smiled Coral, taking the picture. 'Oh, and a new relationship.'

'Or the revival of an old one,' said Marilyn, teasing, smiling again.

'Get in the car.' Coral waved and, biting her lip, turned quickly and walked away, through a crowd of young people coming through the arch.

A BADGE OF SHAME

CHRISTINA DUNHILL

My brother is a good man, though with as much business as three might more conveniently undertake, and a humour to accompany his station. He practises as advocate in the courts of law. It was but two months after my husband's funeral when he sent an offer of accommodation in exchange for such gentle chores as would not fatigue me. I accepted, Reader, after the brief delay politeness demanded, for my circumstances at that time were vexing. Only familiarity with the condition of the poorer classes prohibits me from declaring them of the worst. I was impoverished and with child. My beloved Thomas, the kindest spouse that woman ever wished, had perished with the consumption. We had been married scarcely a twelvemonth and I was more destitute than I could have conceived, still a young woman but grey enough in spirit to feel one with the fog that drifted those days through the streets and courtyards.

When the will was proved, my brother Sidney, as Executor, determined there would be no great sum to my portion: Thomas had bequeathed one allowance to me and another to the poor of the parish; they were of equal amounts and neither was substantial. It was a comfort then to be plucked from the ruins of one life into another where the bustle of maid and cook and frequent visitors seemed to create an impression of robustness against the intemperate winds of fortune.

I moved my belongings into two small rooms at the top of that imposing house in Camberwell and set about my duties: supervising, in effect, the running of the household, reporting to my sister-in-law, Phyllida. In idle moments, I stood at my chamber window, watching the local children running, squealing, at their play upon the common. I knew they would relieve me of my purse as soon as give me good day but their antics made me smile and somehow distracted me from my own approaching delivery.

Having spent his earlier years spreading the gospel overseas, Thomas worked before his death as minister to a poor parish in the north east of London. It was a position which required unstinting devotion, and this constant travail, more in the households of his parishioners than in the Lord's, had wearied him, and left his body susceptible to the harrowings of the disease which later overtook him. I frequently had cause to wish that I had met him earlier in his life when his body was still a match for the youthful zeal of his mind.

Sidney did not forbear to remind me from time to time of my husband's lack of forethought. He had spent his physical energies before marriage in fervent ministry both abroad and at home but yet, in passion incommensurate with one of his failing health, had gotten me with child and neglected adequately to provide for either of us. 'Was this manly conduct?' I steeled my heart against these words because I knew them to be kind in intention. My brother also mused occasionally upon his wife's condition. Womankind was spiritual and angelic, he said, and a constant beneficence in the household. A man's house might as well be made of straw, or he lie in a blanket upon the highway, if it did not contain such a ministering presence. But the more a woman's finer feelings predominated, the weaker and the more distressed would she become if God not give her children.

In fact, my acquaintance with Sidney's wife had not inclined me to admire her. She was a woman of sudden passions, frequently excited by some new company or idea. When she had Sidney's clients to entertain, as was frequently the case, Sidney's presence in the house on his own account being an occasional event, occurring chiefly between the hours of eleven o'clock of a Saturday evening and one o'clock of a Sunday when lunchtime visitors arrived, she was animated. On her own, however, she grew melancholy and would sometimes seek me out, casting a disapproving eye over my papers or needlepoint, and, sniffing hard, pronounce, 'the devil will make work for you soon enough, Elizabeth.' On these occasions I would be invited to her drawing room for what she called a 'communion'. The room was festooned with those penny tracts which tell sensational tales of a quite medieval orientation. Their outcomes are frequently sorry even beyond their incident and how they edify is lost upon me but such is their reputation. Phyllida relished them above all other entertainment and if I called upon her, would engage me in a reading.

I sought what rest I could to garner my strength against the coming of my term and prayed the infant might be a girl to put me less in mind of her father of whom I thought too frequently, gazing upon his likeness in a little silver frame and reading at the book of verses he had left me. I was anxious the child resemble him in few particulars.

Edward St John Thomas was born one dark December day shortly after the evening had closed upon the afternoon. The fog had given way to driving rain and a bitter chill hung in the air. I had all but fastened my heart against him but, and as the good people around me had foretold, he brought me joy. I huddled with him close to the fire and wrapped him in as many shawls as ever swaddled infant. I crooned him little songs and snatches of his father's verses. Then his little cheeks would dimple and his legs would kick. He was as entertaining as babies may be who have somehow divined what hangs upon their humour. And, upon my soul, he looked like no one other than himself.

Even Phyllida was charmed with him. She would dangle him upon her knee and sing him snatches of hymns, or promenade with him clutched to her bosom to display to the servants. My brother appeared delighted with my son and, while I could not but applaud the fine feelings of any my infant enchanted, this caused me some dismay, for I fancied Phyllida resented it, though she said nothing and it may have been of my imagining.

Nothing in the preceding months, however, had prepared me for what next occurred. It was a Sunday morning after church when Sidney called me to his study to confide news of the imminent arrival of a young girl of whom he had been made ward. He had been notified that her boat had docked and she had taken lodgings in Plymouth. He would send a clerk to ride with her upon the railway and escort her to our house. We could expect her arrival inside the week. I was intrigued and should have liked to question him but we were interrupted then by the arrival of luncheon guests which I could not but feel was welcomed by my brother, and I was left to muse alone and anticipate our guest in some little trepidation.

The following Sunday saw her arrival. Sidney, Phyllida, myself and Bertha, the cook, composed a formal welcoming party. All but my brother drew breath to see her as she unbuckled an insubstantial cloak and handed it to the maid, taking pains to disguise her shivers. She could gain a little flesh, I thought. Her name was Selina. She took our hands in turn. Her skin was the colour of almonds, her eyes as brown as a fallow deer's. Her father, I remember thinking, is no doubt some British planter or his importunate son. How came she to be my brother's ward I could not determine.

Over luncheon, Selina told us a little of her story. She had sailed the long passage from the West Indian isle of Jamaica and was relieved to have her feet on land again, albeit in our bitter clime. Her mother had died a year ago, casting her into despondency. Of this good woman she spoke with some awe and a fount of emotion barely concealed by the formal diction and pretty turn of phrase which I soon came to recognize, distinguished her. I fell to wondering if my son would ever speak so of me. She had never known her father but he had purchased her mother's freedom, enabling her to trade in the marketplace and provide for Selina and her half-brother and sister who had all received an education from the mission school. After her mother's death Selina learned that a wardship trust had been created for her, should she choose to take advantage of it, providing for travel to England and board and lodging with an English gentleman and his wife. She had been loth, at first, to leave her native land but a spirit of adventure had always beat within her breast, and, eventually, had prevailed.

She won a place in all our hearts save one. My brother, I could see, was pleased with his ward and went out of his way to make himself available to her. Little Edward gurgled always to see her and would follow her with his eyes, if he was not suckling, and fall asleep in her arms as peacefully as in my own. For my part, I felt the strange flutterings of a dawning adoration. But Phyllida, who might have found in her a sister, seemed to seek to vex her. She suggested dressing her in exotic eastern garb.

'We shall be the envy of Camberwell, she exclaimed, 'with this beauty amongst us. Think how a silken turban will become her, a brocade tunic with gold buttons and skirts of flowing taffeta in the brightest shades. My husband's reputation will increase apace and every day will be as gay as the march past of the black time-beaters in the Worcestershire Regiment.' She smiled upon Selina whose retort I hesitate to set down.

But when Sidney, in whose charge she was, forbade any such frivolity as unfitting for his ward, she suggested Selina might relieve me of the household supervision, so that she and I could devote ourselves to the care of the child. My brother would have none of this neither, saying Selina was but sixteen and had her studies to pursue. She was to be a governess and educate young ladies in the arts appropriate to their station. If we should care to assist her in developing her skill at embroidery, at water colour painting, or playing at the pianoforte, he was sure we would not regret it.

I had begun, I cannot think quite when, to relish the prospect of each day as it dawned. Edward grew most plump and wanton, luxuriating in attention. I remember thinking it was as if some greedy animal who had occupied my shadow had slunk away to look for other fodder. Because of my brother's kindness, I wanted for nothing and need not draw upon my modest allowance.

I spent a good many happy hours with our guest, at the easel or the piano. Her musical gifts were outstanding and her watercolours executed with true draughtsmanship and charm. But when we each relaxed with our needlework, it seemed her mind would set to roaming and then

151

she would debate boldy with an over-agile intellect, as if she had rather politics would be her trade. I am afraid she held little in high regard. I could not but wonder if it was safe for her to have so many British institutions in contempt. On one occasion I was remarking, as I frequently did, upon my brother's great kindness and was dismayed by her sudden rejoinder.

'Mr Sidney,' she exclaimed, 'has talent neither for governing nor growing millet.'

I laughed. 'My brother is celebrated in his profession,' I said, 'and has worked hard to win his reputation. Why, you know how little time he has for leisure here.'

'I do indeed,' she replied, but there was something in her tone which was not an endorsement. 'Your brother labours for his own benefit and his family's; he does not address himself to what is right or wrong. He acts for whomsoever pays his bill.'

Now I have little skill in argument but I endeavoured to explain the intricacies of British justice. I told her how every man who worked within it could set about his own business in perfect satisfaction as to that admirable system prospering the rightful outcome of the whole action, whether it be to the advantage of his side or the other.

She was upon me speedily in tones of outrage: 'Have you not heard tell of men released from the most abject confinement when another has confessed to the crime, or some quite unrelated investigation revealed its perpetrator? What of this remarkable abstract then? It has not revealed the truth; it has not protected the innocent, merely provided employment for its many handmaidens. It protects them well enough. That is the work to which you owe your custody, and think on those who pay the price for it in quite another.'

I exhorted her to watch her tongue. Such sentiments were not for a governess, not for a lady, indeed, were not for decent folk. But privately I wondered. Could Selina's misgivings about my brother's work inform my own as to this wardship? He had vouchsafed nothing further and gave me to understand that I was being impertinent when I made to enquire. I did not dare approach my sister-in-law for her scorn had turned to fear and she wrapped her shawls closer about her when she met our guest on stair or passageway. I knew my brother's dealings sometimes obliged him to incur a debt. Had he been forced into a connection with that despicable traffic: the slave trade? Or with the West Indian plantations whose labour it supplied? I understood this trade had been but little disadvantaged by the withdrawal of British shipping.

Or had my brother a more direct connection with his young ward? I was not aware that Sidney had made any expedition to the West Indian islands but I was in no position to account for every week of my brother's history. When he left home and entered articles he took lodgings north of the river and my mother and I heard little from him until some five years later when he began to practise.

I regret to say Selina herself viewed my evident curiosity with some amusement. If I had ever cause to rebuke her she would proclaim some extravagant heritage in a theatrical rebuttal:

'Be minded who I am!' - drawing an imaginary cloak about her shoulders. 'I am the daughter of Sheba and winged Mercury.' Or another time: 'I am the scion of Hecuba and Lord Mansfield. "Oh England is too pure an air for slaves to breathe in! The notion of perpetual service to a master by a slave is an idea unenforceable at English law."'

She was devilish jaunty and my brother was uncommon fond of her, to be sure. If I had not come to love her so myself, I might have grown resentful. He jested with her; he spoke of the law and the constitution. He procured for her her own set of the complete works of Shakespeare.

One day, alas, Selina was engaged in a spirited imitation of her encounters with my sister-in-law: of how she was able, by sitting on her hands and glaring at a fixed spot, to attain a heedful expression when Phyllida preached from her quaint tracts, how she would affect to be looking for a lost needle on the stair if overcome by the sight of Phyllida muffling herself against her in shawls.

'Blasphemous child, ingrate!' I expostulated, mirthfully, 'To your room!'

'I will relieve you of my company for sure,' she answered, 'and you kiss the hem of my skirts this moment!'

She mounted a little footstool and, raising her eyes to the ceiling, lifted an invocatory hand:

'I am the child of the white god and a sooty daughter of Africé, that great suborned continent whose scattered scions will one day rise to pull the curtain on the sun of your accurséed empire.'

Reader, I curtseyed to her. I adored her and I curtseyed. I was rising to kiss her hand when Phyllida entered.

'As you are both so fond of fiction,' she intoned, 'perhaps you would be kind enough to read to me in my room.'

We dared not meet each others' eye as we followed her and she made her selection: *The True Story of Hetty Ploundgeon: the tale of a woman seduced by the devil upon her childbed.* I had my heart in my mouth when Selina took the paper and raised it in front of her eyes. For my part, I borrowed her method, sat with my hands beneath me and my eyes holding the little ormulu clock on the mantel in a firm regard.

This is a true story, witnessed by me, Maggie Jennings, concerning my neighbour, Mistress Ploundgeon, whose confinement had come upon her suddenly. I was with her at the time, her husband being in another parish, seeking employment. I sent my boy for the midwife but alas, she was too tardy to assist us and my neighbour was in a delirium and began to slash at her own poor body with a knife she drew from the bedding. When I endeavoured to seize it from her, she turned it upon me, forcing my withdrawal to a corner of the room.

She emitted one fierce shriek, then fell silent, and after a little while, began to speak in a strange voice, at once penetrating and winsome:

'Ah, so soon, so soon. I spy the fiend. It is the foul fiend come to claim his own.'

Then, I swear by all that's holy, the devil himself flew into the chamber, shook his shoulders to straighten his cloak, removed his gloves and stood awhile, sucking his claws as he regarded her. He wore a velvet westkit and boots that shone so bright that any but he could see their face in 'em. For his own, ah! it was black as a bison's, albeit narrower in mould, and from his pointed mouth came violet flames. He did not speak but sang in some outlandish tongue. His voice was an effortless tenor and the notes which flowed from his black dog lips as clear as a rivulet, were each encapsulated in a ring of violet smoke.

She called him to her bedside: 'Master Spencer, Master Spencer, come quick!' and, glancing at the fob watch which he took from his left breast pocket, he approached her.

'My time!' she cried, 'my time is upon me!'

Seizing him around the neck, she began groaning again and bore down with all her might. He placed one hand firmly on the bed, braced himself and with the other reached beneath her skirts, lowering his muzzle to her lips. There came then a dazzling luminous flash and when I opened my eyes I saw him lift his head with the cord between his teeth and the shrivelled infant in his hand. He sniffed the air and flew from the chamber. And on the mattress lay nothing but two charcoal stumps.

I did not know whether to give way to laughter or tears after this narrative. But when I glanced at Phyllida, I caught her staring fast at Selina with an expression of unflinching bitterness. Selina held her gaze and her face was steady. Edward began to cry. I said I should withdraw and feed him. Selina too then took her leave and before we were out of the door, she enquired of me loud and boldly:

'Have you heard the tale of my countryman employed in the military band. He was strolling down the Strand when accosted by the question: "Well, blackie, what news from the devil?" With a smart cuff he sent his questioner to the ground, remarking: "He send you that - how like you it!"'

She made her excuses from dinner, pleading a slight chill, and I knew for the first time that she was afraid. I called upon her before turning in but she was deep in slumber. Then, when I had repaired to bed, she entered my chamber and enquired if she might climb in beside me, against the cold.

'Indeed, you may, my darling,' I answered, 'if you are quiet and do not wake him.'

Edward slept in his cot at my bedside. Selina pulled the curtains about us and slid in, putting her arms about my neck like a young child herself, whispering words I could scarce hear but afforded her some merriment. As I felt her shaking against me so I could not fail but give way to mirth on mine own part; and thus we found ourselves giggling like two infants set out to the sun.

It was gone as sudden as it started and left her slumped in quite another humour, leaving me afeared for her, and, strangely, also for myself.

'Are you my sister?' she enquired.

I kissed her. 'In spirit and in faith.'

'For ever?' she continued.

'As God gives me breath.'

Then the tears broke from her and her slight body shook against mine.

'I hate her,' she sobbed, 'and you will soon hate me.'

She twisted free and ran from the room. I lit a candle and followed her to her room where she lay shivering under the finely worked sampler over her bed, with the words SEE NO EVIL worked in cross stitch inside a frame of tropical flowers. I pulled the covers over her and kissed her forehead.

'May God bring you peace,' I said.

But she merely groaned and turned her head from me.

When I returned, Edward had awoken tearfully and it was a while before he was quieted. The following day found him still whimpering and quite out of humour. I wrapped him in blankets and took him to the kitchen where the heat of the great fire was most penetrating, and where Cook and I sorted through the medicaments available and I administered our choice upon my finger. I rocked him and crooned one of his father's verses which I had set to a little melody:

> Take the napkin to your eye
> and staunch those traitorous tears
> which your devotion will belie
> to their beholder. Consign your fears
> to the motion of the spheres. Remember,
> you have my heart and I surrender.

I became aware that Selina was behind me, joining in with the words to a fair approximation of the tune. I broke off.

'You are uncommon gifted,' I remarked, 'to learn a ditty so fast. How is it with you this morning?'

'I am a little better,' she replied, and continued singing.

'How come you to know that song?'

'It is well known, is it not?'

'I would doubt it, it is a composition of my husband's.'

'Then I have heard you singing it, of course.'

I smiled. 'Of course.'

There passed a look between us then which I could not describe.

I sought an early opportunity to visit her in seclusion. I need not have troubled. She had made her way to my own bedchamber where I discovered her rocking my baby's empty cot and holding the little portrait of my husband.

'Tell me, Selina!' I said; my voice was hoarse.

She put the portrait down, still staring at it, and held tight to the cot's bars. Then she fixed me in her red-rimmed eyes and declaimed:

'Elizabeth, I am your husband's daughter. He bought my mother as his maid, and then - perhaps in some confusion as to wifely and domestic service - got her with child.'

'No!' I said. 'He was never in those parts; it is not possible.'

'You must enquire of Mr Sidney then.'

My husband lay with his black slave. I imagined her huge and commanding, taking what she would of him and leaving him spent. I saw him alone, repenting of his sin when the deed was done, and beseeching heaven for forgiveness beneath a tropical sky bright with unreachable stars.

The word was upon my lips but I could not give voice to it. I screamed aloud and ordered her to leave.

'I loved you and you are the badge of my shame!'

She would not move but stood watching me in anger. In her eyes which glinted like black diamonds, I watched fury battle with pain. It was a while before she spoke again, and then in a slow monotone:

'My mother's mother was the eldest daughter of the king of Zoara. She was taken from her homeland by a Gold Coast ivory merchant. When she was fifteeen, she was sold to a Dutch captain for a yard and a half of gingham cloth. He sold her on to a plantation manager in Jamaica; the price then I believe was two guineas. My mother was born on one sugar plantation and sold on at seven years to work in the manager's household of another. Tell me dearest sister, who is the badge of whose shame?'

She was still calm and I was shaking. I wanted to sink to my knees and cry at the hem of her skirt. But it wasn't for her I wanted to cry. Not for her mother or her mother's mother. Nor for the centuries of violent trespass, for all the transgressions; the violation of countless histories and numerous civilisations. All that upset me was my own history moved, for the horizons of what I'd thought my life slipped beyond my grasp.

'My husband...'

She shouted, 'Think not on what you do not know. You insult my mother's memory.'

She left the room.

Because he had not told me. Because he had not trusted me and had not told me. He had another wife. He had a servant whom he'd raped. He had a daughter whom I loved. What kind of man was he, this man of God, my husband and my baby's father?

In the morning Selina was gone. Most unusually, my brother was working at home.

'I understand Selina confided in you!' he said. 'That was premature but cannot be helped. She was disappointed in your reaction. She expressed a wish to be settled in college at once and I have exerted some influence. She will return for a few days at Easter. I trust you will both regain your former spirits then. My wife relies upon them.'

'But Sidney!' I expostulated, 'Your wife...!'

'Enough,' he said, 'I'm late to my chambers. Phyllida would talk with you.'

He is a good man, my brother, but cannot grow millet. I would give my brief to Selina, had I suit to file. How, in due course, she will fare as governess, we shall all be intrigued to learn.

NORA

FRANCES GAPPER

I tracked Nora from Bristol, her home town, around the south coast of England, past Dorset. Then she took off for Europe with her mother and they stayed for a while in Boulogne. Her mother injured a leg, but was still able to fend for herself.

That winter, Nora journeyed south, alone, across the stormy Bay of Biscay and down the west coast of Africa, settling in a fishing port near Cape Town. She seemed to like it there, anyway she made plenty of friends. I was planning to follow her down there, but other things got in the way.

Specifically, my relationship with Igraine - Igraine Hutchinson, the painter. At that time, late 1970s, Igraine was just beginning to experiment with watercolours, and painting 'Sunsets and Balloons', a series that eventually featured in the *Sunday Telegraph* magazine.

We lived in a rented flat in York Crescent - one huge room with three bay windows and incredible views across Bristol to the Mendip Hills. I loved that city. It's strange how you can fall in love with places. In my first year there, I walked in a dream of beauty, around the Georgian terraces of Clifton and the vertiginous tumbledown streets of Clifton Wood and Hotwells, through the winding wooded depths of the Avon Gorge, with the suspension bridge high above, miraculously spanning the gulf. All appeared painted in the softest, most delicate colours. One part of the city was called Fishponds. There was Totterdown, where the houses tottered down the hill, and Bedminster Down, which the local people called Bedme-down.

But my relationship with Igraine. As I was saying, well, in the beginning, we communicated very little. Did I love her, I wasn't sure. It's funny how a relationship can be good sexually, but sort of fade away at the edges, where it touches everyday life. Some days, when she was painting and I was working on my research project, we could have been sitting on opposite sides of the Avon Gorge. Without the bridge.

If I had shown the slightest interest in art, or if she had known anything about the migration patterns of seabirds, we might have got on better. 'It's incredible to me,' she would say, 'how you can spend all day and half the night watching a tiny dot of light move across a computer screen. Don't you get *bored*?'

'That's Nora,' I would reply. 'She's my primary bird. She's spearheading this whole project.'

'But you can't even see her.'

'Yes I can. As clearly as I see you.'

'Ha!' Igraine would make these annoying noises, which I tried my best to ignore.

I could indeed see Nora, in my mind's eye, in my imagination, or rather I could see the world through her. It felt like I was flying, the landscape unfolding below me. The woods, the fields, the ranging southern coastline, the mudflats, the shining water at evening, the misty dawns. I could even see parts of the French coast, places I'd never been. As she flew further south, I would recite the names to myself, a litany - she's passing Lisbon, Casablanca, Agadir, Senegal. She's crossing the Gulf of Guinea....

'You care more for that bloody seagull than for me.'

'Don't be ridiculous, Igraine.'

'I believe you'd love me more if I had wings and a beak. If I was half way across the ocean....'

'Oh, for God's sake.'

Usually Igraine kept her emotions pretty well buried. I'll never understand the artistic personality. We were

161

getting on quite well together, till she started painting those bloody balloons.

When I first met Igraine, she was an alcoholic, and had been one for twenty years. I found that attractive. It meant I wouldn't be asked to cope with her emotional needs, or blamed for them. The whisky bottle would be my substitute, stand-in, alibi. On our second date, she drank orange juice and soda water. I was slightly alarmed, but assumed this was just a temporary blip. I was proved wrong. She was serious about me, she said, and about 'changing'.

She was forty-seven, I was thirty. We sat in the Three Feathers Inn by the Floating Harbour, where they played jazz on Tuesday evenings, and I worried about Nora, who was then just about to hatch. My ex-lover, Caro, was the project leader and she was making things deliberately difficult for me, trying her hardest to get me moved off the nest. Poor Caro, she died soon after that, in a tragic accident. While she was observing Nora's mother and her young brood, she slipped and fell from the rooftop. Luckily no harm came to the birds. Caro would have been glad to know that.

I tried to persuade Igraine not to give up alcohol completely.

'Listen,' she said 'sweetheart, you're the best thing that's ever happened to me. My once-in-a-lifetime chance. I've got something to live for now. Maybe I'll even start painting again.'

'Oh yes, great.'

'Would you sit for me?'

'Sometime, maybe.' I turned and looked straight in her eyes. They were slightly clouded and I sensed desperation behind them. The jazz band was playing a mournful piece, the kind of music you might hear at a funeral, if jazz bands ever play at funerals. Sometimes you can see the end of a relationship, before it begins. I saw our mutual future in her eyes. It looked like nothing but pain. I didn't tell her that, naturally.

'I want to live with you,' she said.

'Fine.'

I'll share living space with you, but I'll never sit for you to paint. You will not capture my soul, naked to be observed. And we'll make love in the dark.

I take credit to myself for the return of Igraine's artistic powers, for don't they say that all great art is born out of deprivation and loss? I deprived her of what she most needed. Me. However, we had a good time in bed. I liked the noises she made there, in the darkness.

Our bed was a mattress covered in a sheet. Lying awake while she slept I watched the moon free-floating above the city, trailing streamers of clouds.

Our project group kept in touch by phone and Computalink with research centres in Europe and Africa. Soon my suspicions were confirmed. Nora had formed an attachment. Seagulls mate for life. Nora had chosen another female seagull, to be her lifelong partner, her soulmate, her joy in flight.

Disaster. I was consumed by rage and grief and disappointment.

Igraine took me to the Berkeley Hotel in Clifton, for lunch. She is enormously generous at the most unlikely times. She ordered a good bottle of wine and made me drink most of it. 'Now why are you so upset?'

'It means the end of the project! The end of everything!'

'Nora's happy, isn't that important to you?'

'But she'll never have eggs!'

'So what?'

'Oh, you don't understand. You've got no idea what this means.'

'So, explain.' Igraine placed her hand gently on mine.

'I've known her since she was a tiny chick. And before that. I watched her hatching, and I made sure she got enough regurgitated fish, and later on I put the ring on her leg, and I've kept track of her for two years ... '

'Are you telling me you're jealous of Nora's girl-friend?'

'I'm telling you she's *mine*. My bird.'

'You can't have sex with a seagull,' Igraine said. A smile flickered across the face of a passing waiter.

'That's not the point,' I said impatiently. 'We still have a relationship, a bond. She can't just go off and leave me like this ...'

Igraine sighed. 'It's a nice day,' she said. 'Let's take our coffee out on the terrace.'

The Berkeley Hotel is built on the edge of the Gorge, above a sheer drop, so I often go there to birdwatch and fantasize. Seagulls drift idly through the abyss, hanging on air currents. The terrace is the roof of the hotel ballroom, white concrete, studded at intervals with round metal objects like overturned saucers; these used to puzzle me at first, until I realized they were the fixtures of enormous chandeliers, hanging below. So if you carefully unscrewed one, choosing the right moment, you could kill someone. Or several people.

I felt deeply depressed. The coffee tasted poisonous, and I wished it were. 'Did I ever tell you about my aunt?' I said to Igraine.

'Your aunt who's a lesbian?' Igraine looked interested.

'She's not a lesbian,' I said irritably, 'she just had an affair with a woman, once. That's an entirely different thing. Well, my aunt was married for twenty years. To a BBC television producer. He was my uncle.'

'You don't say.'

'Listen, will you. I'm telling you this story. My aunt was perfectly happy during her twenty-year-marriage to my uncle. Perfectly happy, on the whole. They lived in Caledonia Square, in one of those big white houses and had a comfortable middle-class lifestyle. Then my aunt got involved in the Women's Liberation Movement, and her husband, my Uncle David, started having an affair with this young girl.

On his production team. With red hair. And so he divorced my aunt, and married this girl. And the bridal procession drove in horse-drawn carriages all the way around Caledonia Square. With my aunt watching from her sitting room window. And she was terribly upset. She never recovered from it.'

'Is she dead then?'

'No. She's living in St Werburghs. What I'm trying to say is, there are things one never recovers from. Devastating experiences. Like being abandoned by the person you love most.'

'Or the seagull?'

'Yes. Exactly.'

'Sally.'

I looked round and she was crying. Tears slid down her face and fell on the white wrought iron table. She was holding onto the table with both hands, knuckles clenched. As if she might hurl it over the terrace any moment. 'Doesn't it mean anything to you ... ' Her voice was scarcely audible. 'Is it nothing, then?'

'What?'

'Our making love together. How we touch ... '

'But that's different,' I said. 'Igraine, that's a different thing entirely.'

'How is it different?' All the colour was gone from her lips and her face. Igraine went pale very easily, but not like this. A sort of despairing paleness. Nearly fifty, she looked about seventeen. I could have crushed her between my two hands, like an egg. 'How is it different?'

'That's sex. What I feel for Nora is ...'

'Love?'

'No, don't be stupid and simplistic. It's nothing to do with love. It's a sort of higher bond - a *blutbruderschaft*.'

Her eyes met mine. Now free of the alcoholic clouds, they were clear green and vulnerable.

'I hate Nora,' she said.

'Well, I hate your bloody paintings.'

'Well, fuck you then.' She got up, searching in her dungaree pocket, slammed down some money on the table and walked out - leaving me with a pile of small change and a seething mix of emotions. And a £50 note.

I stared at the note. It was green and brown, with swirling patterns and a picture of Sir Christopher Wren.

Despite the early spring sunshine, I began to feel very cold. I sensed the imminence of loss. Of losing Igraine. Two years before, this would not have mattered.

I walked slowly up the steep hill from the hotel to the suspension bridge. The bridge is mainly for traffic, with narrow walkways on each side. It was designed by Isambard Kingdom Brunel. In a high wind, it swings about. It was windy that day. The bridge is a well-known suicide point, especially for students, the Samaritans have got a notice up and the council have put spikes part-way along the sides, to stop anyone falling on the main road below and damaging a car. But you can jump from the middle, into the river.

I leant against the side, looking over. A Victorian father once threw his whole family over this bridge, wife and four children. They survived.

Who needs a family? Who needs sex, I told myself. I can sleep alone.

Without her.

But how?

Trying to imagine. I supposed it would be possible. Anything is possible. I'll find somebody else.

But our bodies fit together, know each other. By touch, sense, smell. It's like we've grown into one another's corners. The boundaries disappear sometimes and we feel like one person. I'm not sure who's lying on the bed, or walking across the room.

Tears blurred my eyes and the view went out of focus. Nora and Igraine. I lost my bird, I lost my girlfriend. I loved them and they both abandoned me.

'Sally?' A tentative touch between my shoulder blades.

'Igraine, I love you,' I say quickly, before caution and resentment can take over.

She's smiling, although her face is still marked by tears, and her fine hair is blowing silver in the wind. 'Okay, then stop it.'

'Stop what?'

'Stop giving me a hard time.'

'About Nora - I didn't mean ...'

'Nora is no good for you. She's a flighty young thing. A cold-hearted bitch of a bird. Anybody could tell that. I'm more intelligent and more talented. And richer. You'll find another seagull, plenty of other seagulls. Please don't kill yourself.'

'I had no intention of killing myself.'

'That's good ... ' She kissed my lips, a touch light as feathers. 'You know Sal, it's our anniversary. I fell in love with you not far from this bridge, exactly two years ago. We went walking together in Nightingale Woods and I climbed the Observatory Tower. I could see you through the Camera Obscura, but you couldn't see me. You were sitting on the grass, with this serious look on your face, watching some seagulls flying around. I wanted to paint you. Even more, I wanted to get a hold of you. There was something that fascinated me about you, that was always eluding me, like moonlight or a shadow. I knew then that I would wait for years, or however long it took - you know how the song goes -

> *Seven long years I've waited for thee*
> *Wilt thou not hear and turn to me ... '*

Her arms encircled me and I felt like a bird, gently captured and held. 'Igraine, I'm sorry. I've been awful to you. I don't deserve you at all. Thank you - I mean for waiting.'

'It was a pleasure.'

TIGER, TIGER

MARY BENTON

It was a long time since I'd been in a joint like this. In fact, after several rather unsavoury and discomfiting experiences, I'd vowed never to go near one again. From the outside it looked like an ordinary pub, an ordinary pub with hulking beer-swilling men leering at whatever woman crossed the threshold (except it had been a long time since any man had leered at me, well apart from in the heat of the summer when I had ventured out in a skirt and a cruising driver, disregarding my cropped hair and disinterested expression, had whistled at my hairy legs). There must be something more to the place - yes, over to the side, an opening. A staircase leading down, down to the secret place where only women go, down to the depths of women's sexuality. A shiver greased its way down my spine. I could see myself pressing the bell, eyes on me through the lookout, all eyes on me as I staggered across the floor. I shook myself. 'You'd be so lucky!' Val would say. Why hadn't I arranged to meet her somewhere else, her place, a cafe, anywhere but here?

Gripping the rail, I forced myself down the rusting iron steps. Not a soul in sight. My hands were clammy, my heart skipping out of my chest. I was back five years, my first intrepid entry into the scene. Spurred on by a friend who had said, 'Right, you're gay,' (straight women didn't use the word 'lesbian' then). 'What are you going to do about it?'

I had ventured out to a bar I had gaspingly gathered from a phone line was where I might meet women like me. The same separate side door, the thick door through which I should pass to my other life, my other being. I had stood, my heart in my shoes, unable to make that step. Suddenly the door had been thrust open; a large woman in denims had brushed past me and immediately turned round and started looking me up and down. Help, is she going to devour me, worse think I am not worthy, too femme, too nervous to warrant her attention. 'Yes, this is the women's bar,' she had smiled and let me follow her in; she then became absorbed into the mass of women.

I was left inside the door, wanting to look around, take it all in, too scared to lift my gaze off the near wall, to focus on any woman. The bar, yes I could manage to get to that, to squeeze in, to squeak an order for half a pint. A quick glance around: tables with women sitting at them in twos, threes, where the hell was I going to sit. Hang onto the bar, brace yourself against it, my arm was white with the effort of holding on, trying to stop it trembling. Women talking, dancing, exuberantly, exultantly. It was too much, this energy, too delicious, delirious. Sip your beer, do something with your hands. I had raised my glass, spilling splashes over the bar, aware of women all around, women in thick biker jackets, women watching, smiling.

One sidled nearer. 'It's all right, we won't bite.'

Another was coming in from the other side. I was surrounded. Her eyes met mine, pure unadulterated lust oozing from them. 'You been here before?' Her breath sounded thick in my ear. This was surely what I was here for. 'What's your name, honey?'

I had turned and run. But that was five years ago, when I was desperate to meet someone, anyone, when it was all so new to me. Now I had plenty of lesbian friends, now I just wanted a good time with my mates.

Footsteps behind me, getting louder, heavier, stopping behind me, then an arm thrown around me. I couldn't even scream.

'Liz! You look as if you've seen a ghost.' I turned, and found myself gazing into Val's twinkling eyes. 'Come on in.'

So we entered. A large rambling place with many alcoves, seedy faded decor, a wooden floor, and all the women. Although it was early, some were already swaying on the huge dance floor, others were engaged in animated conversation whilst others assumed standard poses around the bar.

Val was introducing me to her friends, some whom I had seen around before, others who were completely new. 'And this is Marguerita.' I looked, and drew back from the force of her eyes, dark mysterious wild cat's eyes, Tiger, Tiger Burning Bright in the Forests of the Night; those eyes were directed at me. Or did she look at everyone this way, did her eyes glow regardless of the object of their focus? Now she was talking to me, asking me something about my life, my job, how I came to know Val. Her voice was low, throaty; her eyes gleamed mischief, gleamed danger. I was under their spell, could only gaze and burble.

But we were not to be left in peace, well hardly peace, more raging tumult. I was suddenly aware of a presence, a bony presence, invading my space boundaries; everything about the woman was sharp angles, from her high cheekbones and long pointed nose to the bones protruding out of the holes in her t-shirt. As I gaped, she sidled over to Val and breathed at her, 'Who's that tall cool blonde with you?' flicking her head at me. Me? Val looked from one to the other of us and burst into laughter. The woman was not amused.

'How say we move it to the dance floor?' Her eyes bored into mine.

'Eh, not just now, thank you, I, er, I'm busy, er, drinking my beer,' I stuttered.

'I said the dance floor.' It was an order. Marguerita, grinning broadly, had moved away, leaving me with this woman's hard cool stare. I followed my usual tack, give in rather than argue.

'All right, one dance.'

The woman was guiding me, pushing me towards the dance floor, where she attempted to grasp me close to her wiry frame. I tried to wriggle free but found myself pinned tighter; this woman might look slight, but she had plenty of strength in her arms.

'Anyone ever told you you look like Bo Derek?' She was breathing in my ear.

'No, not at all,' I gasped. Bo Derek indeed!

'You got a car? Found it tricky getting here, I bet. I'm an expert navigator, reckon you could do with that.' This woman wasn't wasting any time. 'How say you and me take a little ride back to your place?'

I was staring frantically around; out of the corner of my eye I could see Val and her mates having hysterics. The music finally switched; I had to make a move before it was too late.

'I must get back to my friend, she doesn't like being on her own,' I gulped; how banal can you get? How I extricated myself from her grasp I don't know: head down then backwards dive, then I was away, scampering back to the haven of my friends. The Tiger was nowhere in sight.

'You should have seen your face!' laughed Val.

'Fat lot of help you were!' I snorted, 'I could have been whisked away!' Out of the corner of my eye I could see my dance partner adopting the same approach with a stocky woman with long blonde hair, who appeared to be lapping up the attention. I grinned at Val. 'Yeah, I must have looked pretty ridiculous; I can't cope with anyone coming on that strong.'

After that little bout of excitement I was needing another drink. Exhorting Val to sound the alarm if Bony came near again, I moved towards the bar. Of Marguerita I did not speak, could not trust myself to say her name.

I eased my way through the crush near the bar, a crowd of women, pushing, shoving. A nudge in the ribs. Not that woman surely.... I spun round and met the big black glasses of Jean, Jean who I'd tried to seduce when I was consoling myself on bacardi after the last love of my life had moved on to other things. She smiled at me, but there was a curl to her lips; hell, I must have really made a fool of myself.

'Still knocking back the booze?' she queried.

'Oh, no, I don't make a habit of that. Eh, look, sorry

about last time, I was....' I suddenly realized it was hardly complimentary to inform her I'd only been interested in her because I was really out of it. 'I, er, I'm not usually that crass. Sorry.'

Her eyes cleared; she started to look interested. 'Well....'

'Excuse me,' I gulped, moving away. *What is it about tonight, why is everyone staring at me, what am I exuding?*

It was then I saw those eyes again, burning across the room, meeting mine and flashing. I melted. If you come over here, I will not be responsible for my actions, will fall at your feet, will ... But she had turned away again.

Pull yourself together, she looks like that at everyone. No, that look was special, seared into the essence of my soul, that look could summon up the depths out into the open where they could be freed, empowered. I could see the sea rising and falling, the waves surging; I wanted to rise and soar, dive into her oceans, her deep caverns.

'Want a crisp? Liz?' I attempted to jolt back to reality, to Val's amused look. 'Your friend seems to have disappeared. Fancy a dance?'

Disappeared? She can't have gone when I've said nothing, done nothing to indicate how essential to my existence she is. Feverishly glancing around, I spotted Marguerita over at one of the tables, chatting animatedly. 'No, she's there,' I breathed with relief.

I saw Val's puzzled look, her glance in the direction of my eyes. 'Oh, Marguerita, no I meant that woman who lured you onto the dance floor.'

I felt my cheeks on fire, the hot flush oozing over my neck and ears, and turned away, not trusting myself to speak, disclose the tremor in my voice.

We moved towards the dance floor. A good stomp revived me; now I was ready for anything. Walking towards the side, I turned towards Val, to find myself eyeball to eyeball with Tiger Eyes. My knees buckled. Don't be stupid, talk to her, ask her anything, her hobbies, where she lives, who she knows here. Yet somehow it did not seem the place for trivial conversation. We were on a far deeper plane, I wanted us out of this place altogether, somewhere where we could be wild and free, discover the wonders of the cosmos together.

Hell, she's said something to me, she's waiting for my reply. *What an idiot I must seem, a swooning lovesick wretch.* Trying to speak, I came out with something stilted, formal, could not trust myself to let any emotion through or the whole lot would come splurging out, she would have it all, all my suppressed passion. Then that really would scare her off. Oh, she's going anyway, thinking I'm disinterested or else sensing the inner turmoil. Say something, anything, to hold her here. No, she's gone, moving over to another of Val's friends. I took a huge gulp of beer and cursed myself.

'I was thinking of getting tickets for that play at the Oval House next week; wanna come?'

I turned to Val. 'What? Oh yes, great.'

'When then?'

'Oh, anytime, yes, fine.' *Oh Marguerita why didn't I say something coherent to you, anything just to keep the conversation going, anything to make you think me interesting enough to stay with for a while?*

But something else was happening, over by the door; women were gathering, shouts were resounding. I moved across, then stopped dead in my tracks. Three men were invading, forcing their way through the entrance. Several women, still calm, were trying to reason with them; trying to impress on them this was a women-only space, there was nothing for them here. As I watched a man grabbed one by the hair, forced her head down on a table. Something inside me snapped and I was hurtling across the room, howling at the top of my voice. I had time to see the man release the woman and step back surprised, then I had him with a sharp hook up under the nose, a strong knee in the groin, followed by a further punch to the side of the head. As he crumpled I turned towards the other two, screeching my rage. Rage for all the women who had been abused, misused by men, rage at myself for all the times I had stood by and let things happen, rage at the lovestruck fool who was unable to establish any sort of rapport with Marguerita. Then Marguerita was at my side, by my side, ready to join in, with me, for me. The men were scurrying away.

I turned towards her, saw the glint of approval in those dark gleaming eyes. 'I wouldn't like to get on the wrong side of you,' she smiled. I felt myself go dizzy. Her eyes were now glowing tenderness, concern. The build-up of tension exploded around me; I collapsed into her arms, aware only of my heart pounding furiously, of her strong arms holding me tight, of the desperate yearning for her never, ever to let me go.

But then she released me and my fragile senses were assaulted by the loud buzz of other women, most praising, some doubting, as some always do, mumbling that we should not resort to violence, degrade ourselves to their level. 'They' would be waiting outside now with reinforcements. The evening had come to a premature end. Marguerita was organizing lifts and taxis, ensuring that no-one had to leave on their own. *Hell, she's not interested in me, just whatever needs doing at the time, whoever needs most support. Why had I imagined that look was just for me. When was I going to grow up, stop being mesmerized, infatuated by a look. Take a deep breath now, cool it, build up your defences.*

I was aware of Marguerita's deep voice at the back of my head: 'Have you got a car?'

I turned to her slowly. Did she just want to know if I could get home safely. Or was there more to it? I looked into those dark glowing eyes, and knew for once I had to seize life by the throat.

I glowed back at her. 'Yes, how say we take off into the night together?'

It was barely discernible, the shift in her face, a certain narrowing of the eyes, their metamorphosis from bright to smouldering. Her cheek muscles twitched, she turned away. She was surely not nervous, this magnificent woman, nervous of me? Then her eyes met mine full on. The words were simple, but the smouldering coals promised the fire beyond.

'Yes, why not?'

I staggered in front of her towards the door. Had she really said yes, yes to little me? No, I was not little, I had just saved the day at the club, I had asked her out, I was mean and tough. I thrust my shoulders back, my chest out and threw the door open.

A restraining hand on my arm, a restraining hand that sent a tingle through my whole being. 'Be careful, Liz, there may be pricks outside waiting.' Well, in my present mood I could tackle anything. I looked at Marguerita and beamed. She glowed back, then looked away. I still could not believe it, that she was really here with me. I wanted to leap into the air, to shower her with kisses. No, that was for later.

Later? I thought as I fumbled with the lock. How was I going to get to that stage? As she settled down I stole a glance at her; she lowered her eyes then looked up and smiled from under her long eyelashes. Hell, she was expecting me to make the first move. What should I do? Well, for a start, in the process of showing her how to operate her seat belt I could operate the catch that would propel her seat backwards into the reclining position....

What was I thinking of? I was a good lesbian feminist, I would talk to her, get to know her as a person. I turned towards her, and came face to face with a large nose squashed against the window; the same large nose I had implanted my fist on less than an hour before.

'Lock your door!' I screamed, and she reacted just in time as the door handle was seized. I powered my mean machine into action and accelerated down the street. Glancing in the mirror I noted with pleasure the force of the movement had thrown Matey off balance into the gutter.

I was glad of the power, of the style of my car just then. I'm not that into status and material possessions, but I do like some wheels with a bit of go in them. I turned triumphantly to Marguerita, but she seemed slumped in her seat; perhaps the excitement was proving too much for her.

As I watched she extricated a bottle from her pocket and took a swig. I didn't blame her; if I hadn't been driving I'd have felt like something strong myself.

Where was I taking her? We had reached Holborn, were travelling down Kingsway to the Strand. I had no idea where she lived. The words 'My place or yours?' formed on my lips but I managed to resist them.

'Fancy a walk by the river, blow a few cobwebs away?'

She looked at me with raised eyebrows, then shrugged and nodded. I parked in a space on Waterloo Bridge. The moon was full, casting shimmering lights on the water; I ignored the mud banks and piles of litter on the side, and started to feel romance in my soul once more. Turning exultantly towards her, I started to enthuse about the setting. Her eyes seemed to glimmer through me, not quite seeing me. 'You all right, Marguerita?' Her gaze fixed on mine; it was no longer just deep and mysterious, there was something almost manic about it. I felt a shudder go through me. What did I know about this woman? Was she high on something?

'Sure, I'm fine, just a little tired.' She managed a grin, then produced the bottle from her pocket and offered me some. I glanced at the label, vodka, and shook my head. She took a long swig and replaced it carefully.

As we negotiated the steps down to the South Bank, she staggered and grabbed hold of the rail for support, then straightened up and walked stiffly down the remaining steps. We stood together in front of Queen Elizabeth Hall, watching the water rippling, the loops of lights along the riverfront, the boats illuminated on the opposite bank. The dulcet sounds of a flute mingled with the screech of seagulls. She turned towards me and smiled; my heart started thudding uncontrollably. She ran her fingers gently down the side of my face, down onto the side of my neck; my stomach fell to my feet. Her eyes were fixed on mine, mesmerizing. Oh, they were wild, exciting. She pulled me towards her. My body was responding to her presence, her vibes, crying out yes, this is what you want. But my mind was clear, sharp as a knife, a knife niggling in my guts warning trouble, danger; those eyes were just a little too wild. Then her mouth was on mine, her tongue exploring deep.

I waited to feel the surge of reciprocal passion, to be transported out of myself, merged with her. Instead I felt an outsider, clearly observing the situation. What was wrong? Was it the stale smell of nicotine and vodka fumes, or was I expecting too much? I drew back and looked at her glazed-over eyes. Hell, she was beautiful.

She was gazing at me, smiling. 'It's getting a little *chilly*.' Chilly? I was *red hot*. 'Should we go back to my place?'

How could I resist? At her place passion would reassert itself, it would all be one glorious merging.

'Yes,' I managed, 'I'd like that. Where do you live?'

Before she could answer a bloodcurdling howl resounded round the embankment. 'Harry, they're down here, let's get the bitches!'

Two of the men who had invaded the bar started charging along the bridge to the steps. There was time only to see Marguerita's fist like mine was clenched, her whole body was rigid. Could we handle them? And now another car was dispersing its load of burly drunks. The hairs stood up on my neck. Too many to fight, and this time these men were angry, had the upper edge on us. The car? They were between us and our getaway wagon.

'Under the bridge, out of sight!' I gasped, as we ran towards the bookstalls on the riverfront. The coloured lights of the National Film Theatre beckoned; was it still open? Yes, people were emerging. 'Let's get where there are people - the NFT!' I cried.

In through the glass doors, in amongst the throng of culture vultures in the bar area, hiding in their midst. Peering round the body of one man holding forth on the inner meaning of a film he had just seen where there was practically no action, I spotted the men prowling the Embankment.

'They'll be in here soon, the loo!' I whispered. We

slunk through to the hall, ran down the corridor towards the welcome figure of Frankenstein, and collapsed on the floor in the Ladies.

Marguerita was trembling; I put my arm round her. 'My God, how are we going to get out of here!' she cried. 'Get the police?'

'Oh yeah, and they'll probably do me for attacking them, not to mention being over the limit,' I retorted. 'Let's wait here, they may get tired and go home.'

We sank down by the wall, and waited.

The last film's audience was spilling out, women were coming in and gazing at our dishevelled state, some turning away as they did on observing the young with their placards 'Hungry and homeless' slumped on the concrete outside. At last, a familiar face.

'Louise!' I hissed. 'These men are after us, could you do a reconnoitre outside?' After an initial gaping, she was prevailed upon to venture outside, coming back to report no sign of any heavies lurking.

'Perhaps they've really gone,' I sighed.

'Perhaps they're waiting by the car!' Marguerita shivered.

'Well, we can't stay here all night.' They've probably slashed the tyres so we can't make a getaway. Or perhaps they were too drunk to spot the car? No, don't be naive, they followed us here.

We crept out into the restaurant area and peered outside. The Embankment was illuminated, only signs of cinema-goers and one man bashing away in the dark at weird shapes of metal. A large crowd were walking towards the door, engaged in animated conversation; they turned right towards the steps up to Waterloo Bridge. 'Come on,' I breathed, and we slunk into the middle. Up the steps, I peered out onto the road leading across the bridge; yes there was the car, and it seemed clear. I clutched the keys between my fingers and approached tentatively. People were still around us. No sign of any damage, no body waiting on the back seat. As I clicked the key in the lock there was a thud behind; oh

God they haven't been waiting under the car. My blood froze, and I swung round.

'It's only a cat, let me in!' cried Marguerita, then we were in and away. How could we have been so stupid as to wander round the river when we knew men were after us?

'Where to?' I gasped when I could speak.

'Mortlake, keep going, then right.'

'I think I'll do a few detours to be on the safe side,' I responded, weaving back and forth across the river until I was sure we had shaken off any pursuer. 'Is it all right behind?' But Marguerita had slumped in her seat. 'Marguerita!'

She shook herself and squinted backwards. 'Can't see anything. Hold on, what's this?'

A car was coming up close behind, lights flashing. It tore past, horn blaring and on into the night. 'Just some macho wanker trying to overtake,' I gulped, and drove on.

The sky was a mass of movement, the moon creeping behind the clouds then bursting forth to illuminate the universe, us. Could I take any more excitement tonight? Yes, I must seize hold of this opportunity for passion, for living; recovery could wait for another day.

Marguerita was mumbling to herself. 'What did you say?' I queried.

'Oh, nothing, I just must have dropped my vodka when those bastards came on the scene. No matter, I've got more at home.' But it did seem to matter, she was restlessly edging round in her seat. Did she really need to keep drinking in order to contend with me? Surely I wasn't that threatening.

She said she lived not far from the river; I imagined a grand old house. She was directing me down a side street; the dank river smells blended with the sweet aroma from the neighbouring sewage works. 'Here.' A grand old house, but certainly one that had seen better days; boards over windows, crumbling entrance, the pillars looking as though they could scarcely support the surrounding structure.

'Now where did I put my keys?' She ferreted in her shoulder bag. Turning the whole thing upside down, she sent flying a mass of papers, scraps of hanky and gunged chewing-gum, cigarettes and a comb thick with a substance similar to motor oil. 'Here we are,' she finally exulted, scooping up the heap and hurling it through the front door. 'I'm on the ground floor, not far to stagger.'

I could hardly get inside the front door, the hall was so jammed with boxes, bicycles, ironing board and clothes dangling from every conceivable hook or surface. Somehow this didn't fit my image of Marguerita. She was looking over at me, smiling. 'Well, come in, take off your coat. Just throw it on the floor.' Looking for available floor space, and finding only layers of orange peel and empty drink cans, I deposited my coat on top of the bicycles and tried to wend my way into the next room. What sort of person would live in this pit?

I needed to get into some space of my own, consider my next move. 'Can I use your loo?'

'Sure, first on the right.'

I opened the door and stepped straight onto something squelchy on the floor, and emitted a shriek.

'Oh, sorry, forgot to warn you the cats use it for their toilet too,' called Marguerita.

It looked as if they had been using it for the last week without anyone clearing up the contents which rose high in the litter tray and spread over the bathroom floor. The stench alone would have turned the strongest stomach.

I staggered out to be confronted by Marguerita teetering towards me. 'Come here,' she breathed. Something propelled me forward, but fascination was rapidly being superseded by disgust. As she raised her lips to mine, her eyes glazed over one final time and she collapsed on the floor.

It took some time to circumnavigate the debris with her dead weight, pulling her towards what I judged would be the bedroom. As I crashed the door open, a tousle-headed figure shot out of bed and advanced towards me, heavy object in hand.

'What the hell do you think you're doing?' When she caught sight of Marguerita's prostrate form the snarl turned to a grin. 'Out of her head again? I'll help you carry her next door, she doesn't belong in here. I dunno, all these sweet young things she brings back! Shame!'

I made my getaway, with great relief but a tinge of sadness; how had my gut feeling let me down so badly? Well, in future I'd stick to friends, forget all this grand passion, it just wasn't worth the energy.

A week later Val was ringing me up exhorting me to go to the club with her and her mates. Apparently I was in great demand, they all wanted to see this woman who had saved the day when the club was invaded. I felt a surge of pride; yeah, there were some things I could do.

Val introduced me to her friends. One woman was very solicitious, asking how I was after my ordeal, how I'd managed it. She had soft green eyes that glowed tenderness. As I talked to her I thought what a nice supportive woman, felt something intangible deep inside her that pulled me towards her. This time I would get to know her as a person first, this time I would take my time. There was a sensuous vulnerability around her eyes that made me reach out to her, her gentle tones caressed my soul. This time I would not be a lovestruck wimp; this time I would be strong, an equal. I gazed transfixed; this time I had really found the woman of my dreams.

WRITER'S BIOGRAPHIES

MARY BENTON
Born in rural Lincolnshire, she dreamed of being a wild rodeo rider but ended up picking wild oats and picking bad
peas off conveyor belts. Now lives in the big city (south London), earning a crust working in the voluntary sector. While
writing classes and groups have encouraged her to take
writing seriously, this melodrama group was pure fun; though
she has yet to drag any of her co-writers onto the squash court.

CHRISTINA DUNHILL
Christina Dunhill lives quietly behind net curtains in a small
terraced house in North London but is still hoping to make
it to the prairies.

FRANCES GAPPER
Frances Gapper does not live in a lighthouse or a castle. She
seldom quarrels with her lover and has never killed anybody.

TARA RIMSK
Born Poland 1909. Enjoyed Bohemian existence in Paris during the 1930s, where she frequented literary salons. Became
renowned as an artist, writer and dancer.

      Partnered Nijinsky several times during her spell
with the Bolshoi Ballet. Continues to live up to her reputation as painter, writer, lover and embroiderer of tea-cosies
which she bestows liberally on friends and enemies alike.

HELEN SANDLER
Helen Sandler is an attractive young dyke with a brilliant
sense of humour and a strong political consciousness.

SELECTED SHEBA TITLES

If you've enjoyed this book, why not try Sheba's other lesbian titles. Some are listed below.

You can buy SHEBA books from any good bookshop or order them direct. Just send a cheque or postal order, including 75p p&p for each book ordered, to SHEBA FEMINIST PUBLISHERS, 10A BRADBURY STREET, LONDON N16 8JN. Or call 071- 254 1590 for our free catalogue.

Serious Pleasure
Eds. The Sheba Collective

Exciting, stylish, daring and controversial, this collection marked the beginning of a new era in lesbian history. Still in popular demand two years after first publication, these stories explore the complexities and intimacies of lesbian sex, desire and sensuality.

£6.99 ISBN: 0 907179 42 8

More Serious Pleasure
Eds. The Sheba Collective

Following on from the runaway success of SERIOUS PLEASURE this second generous helping of stories and poems is guaranteed to tempt you. As well as the best of the original writers, including Fiona Cooper, Jewelle Gomez and Barbara Smith, *More Serious Pleasure* features many new, talented and arousing story- tellers. This volume is bound to thrill and delight the adventurous reader.

£6.99 ISBN: 0 907179 52 5

Girls, Visions and Everything
Sarah Schulman

It's summer in New York city; the streets are sizzling. Below 14th street the girls at the Kitsch-Inn are hard at work on their new lesbian version of *A Streetcar Named Desire*. A spirited, funny and affectionate portrait of a neighbourhood and a circle of women holding their own in an increasingly crazy world.

£6.99 ISBN: 0 907179 58 4 Available: October 1991

The Sophie Horowitz Story
Sarah Schulman

Sophie Horowitz, intrepid reporter chasing a scoop for *Feminist News*, finds herself hot on the trail of a group of radical feminist bank robbers. Armed with unanswered questions, Sophie meets the eccentrics and has-beens in the sleazy downside of lower east-side New York. Another triumph from the author of bestselling *After Delores* and *People in Trouble*.

£5.99 ISBN: 0 90719 54 1

People in Trouble
Sarah Schulman

This novel tells the story of an unusual love triangle, and how activism transforms lives. With startling originality

Schulman's novel compels us to confront what justice and compassion really mean.

'This is the first work of fiction I've read about AIDS that portrays the enormous activist response the epidemic has generated... Schulman's people are fighters... terrifically inspiring examples of the human spirit's passion for revival.'
David Leavitt

£5.99 ISBN: 0 907179 53 3

After Delores
Sarah Schulman

This is a story of jealousy and revenge, where identities are elusive and disturbingly fluid. Set on the streets and in the parks and tenements of Manhattan's Lower East Side, *After Delores* is the story of a murder and the loss of love. A thriller with a twist.

£4.95 ISBN: 0 907179 51 7

The Flying Hart
Claire Macquet

Claire Macquet's stories will tighten your breath as they quietly shock with their subtle exploration of the power of sex to explode so much of what we need to see as real and important. Macquet deals with lesbian love from childhood to old age, the love of peasants and angst-ridden social climbers - struggling for space to breathe.

£5.99 ISBN: 0 907179 55 X

FORTHCOMING TITLES

Ghost Pains
Jane Severance

Without shying away from pain and disappointment this novel sensitively explores the struggles of two girls growing up in a difficult world, where alcohol threatens their survival. *Ghost Pains* is a grown-up book about growing up.

£6.99 ISBN: 0 907179 45 2   Available: March 1992

The Move
Tina Kendall

Tina Kendall's first novel draws the reader into Lee's search for new directions in her life. Is Africa, and ultimately the beautiful, compelling Coletrane, her final destination? An intense and lyrical novel from a black English writer which explores shifting sexualities and love between women.

£5.99 ISBN 0 907179 46 0   Available: March 1992

Excitement
Sexual Stories for the 90s
Eds. The Sheba Collective

A new anthology of stories exploring themes and feelings on the subject of sex in the 1990s. With heterosexual, lesbian and bi-sexual heroines these stories focus on the tensions, dangers and conflicts, freedoms and pleasures which make up the diversity of contemporary women's experience of sex. Risqué, hopeful, daring and exciting reading.

£6.99 ISBN: 0 907179 57 6 Available: May 1992